DISNEY CHILLS

LIAR, LIAR, HEAD on FIRE

by

Vera Strange

DISNEY PRESS

Los Angeles · New York

Printed in the United States of America
First Paperback Edition, August 2021
10 9 8 7 6 5 4 3 2 1
FAC-025438-21176
This book is set in Agmena Pro/Linotype
Designed by Phil Buchanan

Library of Congress Cataloging-in-Publication Data

Names: Strange, Vera, author.
Title: Liar, liar, head on fire / by Vera Strange.
Description: First paperback edition. • Los Angeles : Disney Press, 2021. • Series: [Disney chills ; #5] • Audience: Ages 8-12. • Audience: Grades 7-9. • Summary: Twelve-year-old Hector's family is counting on him to win the Zeus Cup in a race, but when a Greek god offers a deal to help him win, all Hades breaks loose.
Identifiers: LCCN 2020052369 • ISBN 9781368065436 (paperback) • ISBN 9781368065467 (ebook)
Subjects: CYAC: Racing — Fiction. • Family life — Fiction. • Hispanic Americans — Fiction. • Hades (Greek deity) — Fiction. • Mythology, Greek — Fiction. • Horror stories.
Classification: LCC PZ7.1.S768 Li 2021 • DDC [Fic] — dc23
LC record available at https://lccn.loc.gov/2020052369

For more Disney Press fun, visit www.DisneyBooks.com

The dreams that you
FEAR will come true.

1
THE ZEUS CUP

As soon as Hector woke up, he almost wished he hadn't.

The alarm blared, jerking him from sleep and the dream he'd been having about running. His legs felt tired, even though he'd slept soundly the whole night. Running seemed to be the only thing he did lately, even while snoozing.

He groaned and flopped over in his twin bed, feeling the softness of the worn flannel sheets and burying his head in the pillow to block out the alarm. When that didn't work, he flailed around until he hit the SNOOZE button. His legs felt sore from training yesterday. He blinked in the dim morning light.

It wasn't that he had to go get dressed and head to school like most twelve-year-olds—he didn't.

In fact, he didn't have to go anywhere.

Hector was homeschooled, along with his three older brothers, and could take all his classes in his pajamas at the kitchen table. He was the baby of the family, and his brothers made sure to remind him of that fact on a daily basis. He didn't even have to brush his hair—technically speaking—although if he left it alone his father would tease him for being lazy.

His dark locks were curly and thick and grew in every direction as if they had a mind of their own, reminding him of Medusa's snake hair. He'd learned about Medusa in their lesson on Greek mythology and found her fascinating.

Sadly, his hair didn't endow him with any stone-stare death powers.

Major bummer, he thought. Too bad he wasn't a Greek god or demigod.

Or whatever they were called.

His dad's voice shot through his head, wise and stern and amused all at once. *Son, you always need to put your best foot forward. That is . . . if you don't wanna fall flat on your face*, he'd add with a chuckle.

He loved laughing at his own corny Dad Jokes, as he liked to call them.

Hector wasn't sure how combing his hair had anything to do with his feet, but parents could be super weird like that.

He rubbed his eyes, forcing them open. His room was the smallest room in the house since he was the youngest Gomez brother, but it was bright and cozy. He had a beat-up wooden desk, an equally beat-up dresser, and a twin-size bed. As he yawned and stretched, he caught sight of his reflection in the mirror on the door. As predicted, his hair shot out wildly every which way. His brothers' voices echoed through his head.

Wonderboy, did yah stick your fingers in an electric socket?

Uh dork-face, your hair sticking up like that doesn't actually make you taller. . . . You're still just an annoying little loser.

But the truth was, Hector actually didn't mind. He knew they loved him, despite the squabbling and teasing.

Affectionately known as the Gomez Four around town, they could get pretty rowdy around the kitchen table until Dad finally lost his patience and yelled at them to shut it . . . or else.

Usually, the *or else* never actually materialized.

Deep down, their father was a total softie, and they all knew it. The real trouble came if Mom was home and overheard them acting up during homeschooling hours. She was the real heavy in the family.

But usually, his mom was busy running their family's store, Hero's Sporting Goods, located right smack in the center of the Mt. Olympus town square, which boasted one stoplight, a smattering of locally owned stores and quaint restaurants, and an idyllic, leafy park filled with white marble statues of Greek gods, the town's claim to fame.

Well, that . . . and the Mt. Olympus Spartan Run.

Ugh. Hector didn't even want to think about the Spartan Run, but unfortunately, he had no choice. There was no point in delaying the inevitable. Hector climbed out of bed before Mom could yell for him.

"*Wonderboy* . . . yeah, right," he muttered to his reflection.

Sure, on the outside he looked strong and fit and athletic. He'd been training for so long now that he was faster and could do more push-ups and pull-ups than almost any other kid his age, which is what had earned him the dreaded nickname. It also made him the favorite to win this year's Mt. Olympus Spartan Run, a grueling obstacle-based competition for local twelve-year-olds. The annual race was only two short weeks away. It was also the reason for his daily misery.

Hector was finally old enough to qualify for the race, having just turned twelve a few weeks ago. And he did look the part of *Wonderboy*. But inside, he didn't feel strong. He felt weak and unworthy of the Cup.

The Zeus Cup.

Hector pictured the shiny, golden statue molded into the form of the ancient Greek god Zeus. He knew that Zeus wasn't just any god: According to Greek mythology, he was the god of the skies and thunder and the ruler of all the gods on Mt. Olympus.

But that trophy was the bane of his existence. He wished that it didn't exist. Or rather, it could exist, but he wished that his family didn't care so much about him winning it. Making it worse, it wasn't just his family who cared—it was everyone in the whole town.

Winning the Cup was the highest honor in his quaint, idyllic Midwestern town.

Idyllic . . . but boring.

Not much ever happened here—except the race. It was literally the only thing the town was known for. The race itself dated back over one hundred years to the founding of the town by immigrants from Greece. Today, the town was much more diverse than it had been back then, and everyone in his family had trained for the race when they were twelve—his father, his mother, his three older brothers. But they'd all fallen short of winning the prized Cup. His oldest brother, Phil, came the closest, but he finished in second place. And second didn't earn you the Cup.

Now it was up to Hector to win the race and bring the trophy home for his family. But the problem was, he didn't care about winning the Cup. He hated training. He hated competing. He hated pretty much everything about the race.

But nobody had ever asked him what he wanted. Hector would have much rather spent his time working on his true love—photography. Out in nature, snapping landscape photos or capturing candid portraits was when he felt most alive.

A few years ago, he'd discovered his dad's old Canon in the basement, covered in dust, and salvaged it. Ever since then, he couldn't stop taking and developing pictures—experimenting with different shutter speeds and saturations to create new sorts of images. But his family thought that artsy stuff was just a waste of time.

Time that Hector should spend *training*.

Phil was always on his case, pushing him to focus harder on his athletics and not waste time snapping pointless photos of "random stuff" that nobody even cared about.

The problem was, Hector cared. He'd even bought special cleaning products to care for the lens, using the money he saved up working at Hero's on the weekends with his family.

Ugh, I don't wanna train today.

His eyes flicked to the overstuffed athletic bag shoved in the corner and chock-full of gear—sweats, running shoes, special powder to keep his hands dry while scaling walls and climbing ropes. *Hero's Sporting Goods* was emblazoned on the side of the bag, advertising their shop.

It wasn't like he had a choice. After homeschooling was finished, Dad and the boys pitched in at Hero's, helping their mother restock the merchandise—everything from baseballs to lacrosse sticks to rock-climbing equipment and everything in between—and running the checkout counter, then closing up the shop and sweeping the stoop at the end of the business day.

But lately, Hector had to train at the local field every day—and Phil was his coach. Even though he was only sixteen years old, there was no better coach in town. And he drove Hector super hard.

Maybe he could pretend he was sick today?

Like deathly about-to-die kind of sick?

That was unlikely to work, though. His mom could sniff out lies, even virtually over text.

Maybe he could just beg for a single day off? One measly day of rest?

But he knew that wouldn't work, either, not in the Gomez family. Training was the most important thing, even more important than school, though his parents wouldn't admit that, at least not if somebody else was listening. In fact, athletics was the family's business.

Not just their business—but their life. They all lived and breathed and obsessed over the annual race. All except Hector.

Outside his bedroom door, he could hear the house beginning to stir and awaken around him. The squawking of alarms and creaking of stairs and doors. The sound of his older brothers squabbling over who got to shower first.

"No fair, Phil," Luca griped, banging on the bathroom door. "You went first yesterday—and used all the hot water!"

"Lemme alone," Phil's muffled voice shouted back. "I'm the oldest—that means I get first dibs on shower time."

They only had one bathroom for the kids, so it was always a morning battle. Another voice echoed through the house, this one higher pitched.

"Hey, whatta 'bout me?" Juan added to the morning cacophony, his voice cracking.

"You're last!" both Phil and Luca yelled back at the same time.

"Well, except for *Wonderboy*," Phil added, making all three brothers crack up. "We all know he gets a cold shower."

Still in bed, Hector rolled his eyes. Besides, the joke was on them. He'd been showering at night before bed when there was plenty of hot water left.

The smell of bacon drifted down the hall, mixed with the rich aroma of coffee burbling into the coffeemaker. That meant it was banana-pancake-and-bacon day, his favorite day.

Hector stood up and stretched. It wasn't that he didn't have a nice life. He had a goofy, loving family and a comfortable home, even though his large family stretched its limits at times. And his brothers were his best friends.

But there was all this pressure around the race. He just didn't get it. Hector often felt like an outsider in his family. Like he didn't fit in or belong.

When he was younger, he once asked his parents if he was adopted, much to their abject horror. They quickly assured him that while he may have been a "little bit of a surprise," he was definitely their child.

"You're a Gomez, son," his father said, patting his shoulder. "Should I congratulate you—or apologize?"

"Oh, stop it, Pedro," Mom said, playfully slapping Dad's shoulder. "We both know you should apologize."

They each chuckled, not noticing the crestfallen look on Hector's face.

It wasn't that he didn't want to be part of their family. Truly, he did love them. It was just that he couldn't understand why he felt so different.

It was a mystery.

Even his parents seemed baffled at times by his lack of enthusiasm over competing for the Zeus Cup, despite his best efforts to try to fake it.

His eyes flicked to what he truly loved—his camera. It sat in the worn old bag on his desk, labeled *Canon*.

All I want to do is take pictures, but nobody understands me, he thought, feeling . . . well, angsty and misunderstood.

That was his usual state of being, though he tried his best to hide it.

"Hector, you're late for school," Mom called from the kitchen, snapping him out of his usual morning pity party. "Don't make me call you . . . *again*."

"Coming!" Hector yelled quickly.

He knew better than to argue with his mom, especially before she'd had her minimum two cups of coffee.

None of the Gomez Four wanted to be late for homeschool, even though there was no bell to signal that they were tardy—or principal's office to get sent to if they misbehaved.

While Dad was their teacher, a role which he relished and gave his all, Mom functioned as their principal. Suffice it to say, no one wanted to get sent to her office.

With a deep sigh, and before his mother could call for him again, Hector turned away from the camera bag. He got dressed and ran his fingers through his hair, though it didn't help and probably made it worse, and sauntered into the kitchen for breakfast and homeschooling. Hector actually looked forward to the school part of his day. He liked learning new things. What he didn't like was what would come right afterward:

Training. Training. Training.

And more training.

"There's the Wonderboy!" Dad called from the kitchen table. "Looking stronger every day, thanks to your brother here." He clapped Phil on the shoulder, making him wince.

Dad might look like . . . well, a normal middle-aged dad with thinning hair and a paunchy stomach, but he was still almost as strong as he'd been in his teen years when he trained for the race, just like everyone in their family.

"This is our year," Mom added from the kitchen, where she was slurping coffee. Her long, dark hair was tied back into a crisp braid. She was dressed in her usual work uniform—a red Hero's shirt paired with khakis and athletic sneakers with a yellow lightning bolt.

"Yeah, nothing can stop this kiddo," Phil added with a wink. "Plus, he's got a secret weapon that makes him go faster—"

"Yeah, farts!" Luca said, careening into the kitchen and letting out a loud fart sound by pressing his hands to his face and blowing on them.

"I meant my coaching—" Phil shot back, but then Juan cut him off.

"Magical fart powers!" Juan added, giggling like the little monster he was and chasing after Luca in the kitchen while they both made farting noises, trying to outdo each other.

"Stop it!" Mom started, swatting at them.

But she couldn't help it—she snorted a laugh, spraying out coffee.

Then the whole family broke out in raucous laughter. Hector giggled, feeling better already. Just when he felt too much pressure, his brothers always had a way of lightening the mood. Dad slapped the table joyfully, tears leaking from his eyes.

"Oh, these are definitely my kiddos," he managed between chuckles.

"That's right, I blame you," Mom said, trying to sound stern. But her smile betrayed her true feelings. Hector felt lucky to have parents who still genuinely adored each other.

"Okay, enough goofing around," Mom said, getting hold of herself and swallowing the last of her coffee in one gulp. "Time for school—and time for me to get to work.

Somebody has to bring home the bacon," she added, sliding a fresh plate of it onto the kitchen table.

As Hector settled into a chair and opened his workbook, he felt a more serious mood descend over him. He tried to focus on his work, but he could already hear Phil's voice coaching him to run raster, climb higher, train harder.

Phil was even more on edge lately because the last preliminary race was two days away. And the real deal—the Mt. Olympus Spartan Run to claim the Zeus Cup—was in two short weeks. Hector knew he should be excited, but he just couldn't wait for it to be over.

2
MT. OLYMPUS

"**C**ome on, Wonderboy," Phil said, rushing Hector up from the kitchen table the second Dad declared homeschooling finally over. "We gotta hit the field. This is crunch time."

Hector, Luca, and Juan had just finished a lesson on fractions. Hector despised fractions. Math class was his least favorite subject by far, but he still wished that the lesson wasn't over, or that there was some way to delay the inevitable torture that awaited him at the field.

"Yeah, boy! It's *crunch time!*" Juan teased, getting up to give Hector a noogie. "Have fun!"

"Better you than me," added Luca.

He and Juan ran to the living room to play video

games until it was time to head over to the store. They spent every free minute on video games.

Excitedly, Phil grabbed his clipboard, where he meticulously recorded all of Hector's race times. He took his job of coaching his little brother seriously. The times had decreased steadily with each week of intensive training leading up to the big race, thanks to Phil's rigorous coaching and Hector's efforts.

Phil peered back at Hector impatiently when he didn't budge from the table. He tapped his clipboard and checked his digital watch. "Four hours until sunset means . . ."

"*Four hours* left to train," Hector repeated the familiar mantra, his stomach lurching in response.

Slowly—even hesitantly—he stood up from the table, which was piled with computers, the remains of snacks, workbooks, and crumpled homework. It was like his whole body was rebelling against the idea of training today.

Meanwhile, oblivious to Hector's dread, Luca and Juan squabbled over the PlayStation.

"Hey, I go first," Juan said, leaping onto the sofa and grabbing for the controller. His straight brown hair was clipped into a bowl cut. It flopped in his brown eyes.

Hector envied Juan's style. His own hair would never fall that straight.

"No, my turn!" Luca added, shoving his brother out of the way. Luca's hair was styled into a spiky buzz cut with lines carved into the sides like lightning bolts. He liked to call himself Lightning Luca, even though he'd never been that fast.

"You went first yesterday," Juan whined, trying to swipe the controller back. "It's not fair. We have to trade off."

"That's because I'm older," Luca said, snagging the controller back from Juan. He held it up over his younger brother's head, just out of his reach.

"Boys, settle down," Dad shouted as he started cleaning up the kitchen table and clearing away the books. "Or nobody goes first anywhere—except to their bedrooms to be grounded."

Dad chuckled at his own joke, his ample belly shaking. Even though he wasn't in shape the way he used to be when he was Hector's age, the pictures from when he was young looked so much like Hector it was almost eerie. Dad loved regaling them with stories about his glory days of racing, especially over loud, boisterous family dinners.

His year to race, he came in fourth place right behind their mother, who took third place. They both had been so close but so far at the same time.

"Take that, Zeus!" Luca yelled at the television. He and Juan were playing some new fantasy game featuring the Greek gods. They were totally obsessed with it lately. "I'm so gonna take over Mt. Olympus."

No matter what they were doing, everyone in the Gomez family was competitive. Hector jealously watched Juan and Luca jamming at the PlayStation controller. His stomach churned. He wished he could just go in there and join them. Or do what he really wanted to do—wander around outside and snap pictures of landscapes, or animals, or just about anything.

"Can't I play hooky just this once?" Hector pleaded with Phil, feeling the words stick to his tongue, which felt thick in his mouth. "Magic hour is around sunset. It's the best time to take pictures, but I always miss it—"

Phil cut him off. "Heroes don't play hooky. You wanna win that Cup, don't you? You can take pictures another time. We can't afford to slack off right now."

"But please, just one day," Hector said, almost

swallowing the words. "I promise, I'll train extra hard tomorrow."

Dad looked over and met his eyes. "Son, I know it's almost time for the big race. Trust me, I've been there, standing right in your little—I mean big—shoes. It can feel scary. But you know how much this means to our family, right?"

"That's right, we deserve to win that Cup," Phil said, piling on to the guilt trip.

"Yup, and this is our last chance," Dad added, clapping Hector on the shoulder. "You might be the youngest Gomez, but you're also the fastest and strongest. This is our year to win it."

They looked expectantly at Hector. The desire for the Zeus Cup clearly shone in their eyes.

It was true—he was their last chance.

Hector did know how much this meant to them. It had been drilled into his head since he was a baby. Maybe even since before he was born. There was no avoiding his fate—or *Fates*, as the Greek gods called them.

"Of course," Hector forced himself to say. It was pointless to argue.

"The prelim race is in two days, Wonderboy," Phil said, tapping his clipboard. "You have to have a solid finish to even qualify for a slot in the big one. We don't have any time to waste, especially taking boring pictures of lame nature stuff."

"Yeah. Okay."

They don't understand me, Hector thought glumly as he slunk off to his bedroom to grab his athletic bag and running shoes. *They don't even bother to try.* He eyed the camera sticking out of its bag, then reached for it and picked it up, feeling the smooth button that triggered it to snap pictures.

"Hurry up!" Phil called, making Hector almost drop the camera.

He started to leave the camera on his desk, scooping up his athletic bag instead. But then he hesitated.

Maybe I can sneak off and snap some pictures during training.

That thought cheered him up slightly. He snuck the camera into his sports bag, carefully tucking it inside a towel.

As he headed for the door, he caught sight of his

reflection in the mirror. He looked tall and strong—every bit the athlete his family wanted him to be.

But inside he felt different.

He was a Gomez, though, and that meant . . .

Time to train.

He headed for the door and the rigorous obstacle-filled workout that awaited him at the local town field.

* * *

In his beat-up cherry-red pickup truck, Phil drove through the center of Mt. Olympus, a quaint town square filled with local shops and governed by that one stoplight.

Welcome To Mt. Olympus . . . Home Of The Mt. Olympus Spartan Run, read the cheerful sign leading into town.

Hector cringed at that reminder of his future. It wasn't just that he had to get through the race in two weeks. If he did well, he knew that wouldn't be the end of it. His parents would want him to keep training in the hopes of getting a track scholarship to college, just like Phil was doing. The more successful he was in these races, the more hopes would be pinned on his promising athletic career. It was like a double-edged sword.

If he failed, he would let his whole family down. But if he succeeded—if he won the race and captured the Zeus Cup—then the pressure would never stop. But what choice did he have?

Oblivious to Hector's angst, Phil cracked up the radio, bobbing his head to the upbeat rock song. Hector glanced at him.

Phil looked like an older version of Hector. He still had a boyish face, but he was taller, with long, awkward limbs and a curly mop of hair that was shaved close on the sides. It seemed to be all the rage these days on social media, but Hector just thought it looked silly.

"Your haircut makes you look ridiculous," Hector blurted out with a giggle. "You look kind of like a celery stalk. Tall and narrow with curly leaves on top."

"Hey, dude, I look super rad," Phil shot back, running his hands through his hair and primping in the rear-view mirror. Hector snorted out another laugh at his brother's antics.

"Yeah, like a *rad* celery stalk," he quipped. "Not sure vegetables are ever cool, though."

Phil winked at his reflection. "Whatever. You're just jealous of my sick style."

Hector cracked a smile, then turned his gaze back to the window, watching the storefronts flash by as he and Phil drove through the familiar downtown.

Mt. Olympus often felt like a piece of history, perfectly preserved and untouched by modern conveniences and the passage of time, almost like a relic of some ancient era that had long since passed into memory, like out of their history lessons. While that made it a safe place to grow up, it also meant little ever happened there.

Safe meant boring, at least in Hector's opinion. The race was the town's one claim to fame, and the source of all the excitement around these parts. *Cuz it's not like there's something else to get excited about*, Hector thought glumly.

They didn't have a major sports team or even a concert venue. You had to drive two towns over to see the newest movie releases at the multiplex, and even farther for concerts.

Mt. Olympus had the Spartan race.

And that was it.

The thought made Hector's smile fade, and he couldn't help thinking about the grueling torture session Phil had planned for him at the field. He sometimes hated how he could go from fine to annoyed or sad like someone had flipped a switch. His mom said he was moody, and his moodiness had seemed to intensify when he turned twelve. She assumed it was because he was a tween now, and it came with the territory, but Hector knew it was something else. It was the race, and the fact that turning twelve meant this was his year to qualify. It was too much pressure, but he couldn't tell them that.

His eyes landed on their family's store. They had the prime spot in the center of town.

"Hero's Sporting Goods—Official Sporting Goods Supplier of the Mt. Olympus Spartan Run since 1917," read the sign printed on the red awning. The business had belonged to his mom's side of the family, but when she married his father, they'd taken over the day-to-day running of the place. They carried everything anyone could ever want in sports merchandise.

The only thing missing from the store was . . .

The Zeus Cup.

Through the large storefront windows, which were always glistening and spotless (Hector had scrubbed them many times under his mom's careful watch), he saw the empty glass trophy case, prominently placed front and center. This is where the Zeus Cup was supposed to be displayed. His grandparents had it built years ago, hoping someone in their family would one day bring the Cup home.

Unfortunately, it had remained empty ever since.

Hector knew that winning the Cup and displaying it proudly in the front window would bring glory to the family and bump up business for their store, too. He felt the added pressure building inside him like a valve that needed to be released. He did want to win it—not for himself, but for his family. They loved him and took care of him, putting a roof over his head and food on his table.

But he didn't feel worthy.

Inside, he felt weak and afraid.

Mom stepped outside to sweep the front steps as they drove past. She waved at them, grinning at Hector.

"Good luck training!" she called out in her singsong voice. Her long, dark braid swung around her neck. "Break a leg . . . or actually . . . don't break it. But you know what I mean," she said with a wink. Her eyes still sparkled with youthful energy, despite her age.

"Thanks, Mom!" Hector shouted back through the window.

He sat back again and tried to focus on the positives. Like last night, Juan and Luca had slipped him candy bars after dinner, breaking their parents' no-candy-during-the-week rule, because they knew he would be famished from practicing so hard. Apparently, they'd snuck into the pantry and swiped them from the top shelf, where Dad hid his stash, unbeknownst to Mom, who was always on him to eat healthier. Dad had a serious sweet tooth.

Their truck curved around the central town square, which had large marble statues of famous Greek gods. The town's founders had been big on celebrating their history and culture.

Under the leafy trees and scattered among the benches where people lounged and snacked and played with their kids, stood the statues—Zeus, Hera, the Fates, the Muses, Pegasus, Hercules, and of course Hades in the middle of it all. He was the God of the Underworld.

Hector shuddered, picturing the god who ruled over the souls doomed to the River Styx. He'd loved their father's lesson on Greek mythology, partially because it related to their town. He knew the names of all the gods by heart and what they controlled. The Hades statue stood a little bit taller than the others—and he looked creepier, too. It was befitting his role.

Hector's eyes locked onto the statue of Hades. The god had spiky, needlelike teeth and a wicked grin, and wore long robes. Flames took the place of his hair, curling upward into a peak.

Suddenly—*for a split second*—the hair flashed with blue flames. The statue's eyes lit up yellow and locked onto Hector.

They bored into him.

Hector flinched in shock and grabbed his brother's arm. Phil jerked the steering wheel in surprise, and before Hector could blink, with a deafening squeal of the tires, the car veered to the side of the road.

3
EMO GOD DUDE

"**W**atch out!" Phil snapped. "I'm driving here!"

He steadied the truck, but they'd almost swerved into the ditch on the side of the road.

"I'm sorry! But look!" Hector said, pointing to the statue of Hades in the town square.

"What's so important that you almost made me crash?" Phil said with a scowl, squinting toward the park. "I don't see anything."

"Over there . . . can't you see it . . . that tall statue in the middle?"

Hector leaned forward for a better angle, but everything looked normal now. The statue of Hades was just a statue. There were no blue flames. No fire. No smoke.

Nothing.

Hector blinked to clear his vision, but it didn't matter. There was nothing out of the ordinary. And now he felt silly for almost making them crash.

Phil frowned. "Uh, yeah. Hasn't that dumb statue always been there? What's that guy's name again?"

"Hades?" Hector said, his heart still pounding.

My eyes must've been playing tricks on me, he thought, feeling foolish.

That was the only possible explanation. Statues weren't alive, and they certainly couldn't catch on fire. Let alone with *blue* flames. They were made out of marble, for crying out loud. He was probably just stressed out about the upcoming race.

"Yup, that's the guy," Phil confirmed, steering them around the town square. The statues whizzed past their windows. "Lord of the Dead. Or Underworld. Or something super emo like that. Who cares? It's ancient history . . . *literally*." Phil snorted out a laugh.

Clearly, he'd inherited their dad's annoying habit of laughing at his own corny jokes.

"That's right," Hector said, remembering the lesson. "He rules over souls, right? I wonder what other crazy god powers he has."

All the Greek gods had more than one power. It was one of the most interesting parts of learning about them.

"Uh, let's see," Phil said, drumming the steering wheel to the upbeat rock song blaring on the tinny old radio. "I remember something about potions or alchemy. And something else—oh yeah . . . fire."

"Wait, what did you just say?" Hector asked, holding his breath.

"Uh, the emo god dude has fire powers?" Phil said. "Wow, he'd be fun to have at a family barbecue. Wouldn't even need a lighter." He chuckled again.

But Hector wasn't laughing.

Hades had fire powers?

He remembered how the statue's spiky hair ignited with blue flames. That couldn't be a coincidence . . . could it?

Phil glanced at Hector with concern. "Hey, you look a little clammy. Sure you're feeling all right?"

"Yeah, I'm fine."

"Since when do you care about the Greek gods so much?" Phil narrowed his eyes.

"Uh, I don't really care," Hector said, though he still felt unsettled. "You're right, they're lame and boring, totally ancient history."

"Okay, good," Phil said. "That's my all-star. We can't have anything distracting you before the prelims. You have to qualify, remember?"

"Yup, it's crunch time." Hector repeated what had been drummed into him every day for the last few weeks.

"That's right, Wonderboy," Phil said in his best coaching voice. "We've got to train hard if we're gonna win." He paused and frowned. "Trust me, dude. You don't wanna end up like me. Coming in a close second. Always wondering *what if*. That's why I'm so hard on you out there."

"Wait, you still think about your race?" Hector asked, feeling curiosity prick at him. It seemed like an eternity since Phil had competed. Hector had only been a little kid back then.

"All the time," Phil said, setting his lips into a grim line.

"But you came in second," Hector said. "That's really awesome."

"Awesome, but not good enough," Phil said with a sad shake of his head. His celery-top hair flopped around. "You only get one chance to win, and it's gone before you know it."

"But that was four years ago," Hector said. "And you did the best you could."

"Did I really?" Phil said, sounding uncertain. "How can you be sure?"

"Because I saw you race," Hector said, thinking back to when he cheered his brother on from the bleachers with his family. "You barely lost! For most of the race, you led the pack."

Phil reached over and shut off the radio. Silence engulfed the car. "Look, I know I don't talk about it much," he said. "Cuz it's not easy to admit. But yeah, not a day goes by that I don't think about my race—or dream about it."

"Wow, you dream about it?" Hector said. "I thought I

was the only one who ran races in my dreams. I even wake up tired from all that running in my sleep."

Phil laughed a grim laugh. "More like nightmares," he said. "I replay the race in my head all the time, wondering if I could've done something different. Trained harder that last week. Jumped a little higher. Turned on the speed a little more toward the end. Or if it was just my bad luck that day, and I wasn't good enough to win. I came so close that I could almost feel the weight of the Zeus Cup in my hand. So close, but not close enough. That's why I'm so hard on you on that field, my man."

Hector felt that sink in. He couldn't believe how much Phil still dwelled on his second-place finish. As his brother droned on about the importance of focusing on his training, Hector closed his eyes, but he couldn't stop seeing the Hades statue in his mind.

The blue flaming hair. The glowing yellow eyes. Almost as if they were looking into Hector's soul.

* * *

"Stay focused!" Phil yelled from the side of the field. He checked his watch and then smacked his clipboard.

"I'm trying my best!" Hector shouted breathlessly, scaling a rope to the top, then leaping onto a narrow beam. Below him spanned the practice course, erected at the athletic field behind the school so that kids like Hector could train for the big race.

Several different obstacles made up the course. Next up was a towering wall to scale, which always felt hard until he got to the other side and had to clamber down without falling. Then there was a series of ropes to climb, a pit to swing across, and netting to army-crawl under.

Suddenly, Hector wobbled on the balance beam, almost falling flat on his face. *Stay focused*, he told himself sharply, catching his balance at the last second. That was close.

In the practice course, he would have only landed on grass, but in the real race there would be mud traps and more difficult obstacles threatening to trap him. The exact layout was kept a secret in order to make it harder. All the athletes could do was train and hope they were ready for whatever crazy things the race committee threw at them to trip them up. It wasn't like a normal race. It was much more challenging. Not only did Hector have to be swift, but he also had to be clever and nimble. He had to be able to improvise and think on his feet.

"Your best isn't good enough!" Phil yelled back from the sidelines. "Not if we're gonna win the Cup. Try harder, Wonderboy. You don't wanna end up like me, trust me."

"Hey, it's not as easy as it looks," Hector replied defensively.

Or rather, it probably looked pretty hard—but actually racing the course was more difficult than it looked. The obstacles just kept coming at him, faster and faster, every time he practiced.

Hector tried to focus and get past the balance beam. He was breathing heavily as he reached the wall and started climbing, his fingers finding the narrow handholds.

Ring!

In the distance, the school let out. He could see the students from his perch on top of the wall. Kids streamed for the buses or hopped on bikes to head home. Hector felt a familiar sense of curiosity and envy as he watched them. What was it like to go to school with kids your own age, not just your brothers? And sit in a class at an actual desk, not just the kitchen table? While a teacher who you weren't related to taught you math?

And have recess where you could run around outside with your friends?

And be around . . . girls?

Hector wasn't sure what to make of girls. He didn't spend much time around any, except his mother.

But she didn't count.

Hector almost lost his balance at the top of the wall. His foot slipped and his heart lurched, but then he caught himself and started carefully down the other side.

"Stay focused," Phil yelled again, spotting his slip. "We can't afford mistakes, not this close to the race."

"Sorry," Hector managed to get out while gasping for air. He was nearing the last phase of the course, but it was also the hardest part. He wanted to beat his best time and prove he could win.

Hector wove through the next series of intense obstacles—the rope climbs, the pit, the army crawl, and then the hurdles. Phil kept pushing Hector harder and harder.

Just as Hector crossed the finish line, a girl sauntered onto the field, having just gotten out of school. Hector caught sight of her out of the corner of his eye as he fought to catch his breath. Her long, shiny black hair whipped around her tanned shoulders. She wore hip athletic clothes—track shorts and a sleeveless shirt, paired with electric blue running shoes with a golden lightning bolt on the side.

"Mae, hurry up!" barked a man who trailed behind her with a stopwatch and clipboard, just like Phil. "We've only got a few hours left to train."

"Yes, Pops," she said, tying her hair up into a sleek ponytail, then bending down to tighten the laces on her shoes. She cocked her eyebrow and smirked. "I've got the race in the bag. Don't even sweat it."

Hector was mesmerized by her. Something about the way she walked and talked with such confidence. He took a step back to watch as she started the course. She whipped through the obstacles with a grace and ease of movement that astounded him.

"Whoa," Phil said, joining Hector on the sidelines.

"Yeah. She's amazing," Hector said.

While he was fast when he worked the training course—maybe even a little bit faster than the girl—his movements were nowhere near as elegant and smooth. It was like watching a dancer, but one who could scale walls and climb ropes and vault hurdles. He didn't realize his mouth had dropped open until his brother reached over and pushed his chin up. Hector blushed.

Who was this strange girl? And why had he never seen her here before?

"Okay, enough gaping. Your time was good until you got to the wall and lost focus. Let's run it again."

"Yes, Coach," Hector said, adopting Phil's all-business tone. He jogged back over to the starting line, trying as hard as he could not to watch the girl as she made it to the balance beam.

Phil blew his whistle, and Hector took off. He sprinted and jumped, dove and climbed, making sure to focus on what he was doing and not on the people around him. He was kicking butt—he could feel it. And soon enough, he found himself back at the base of the wall.

From the corner of his eye, he saw a flash of movement.

He couldn't tell where the girl was on the course, but she was close by.

Stay focused, he told himself, hearing his brother's voice in his head. *Don't get distracted.*

He dug his feet into the turf, sprinted down the field, then leapt halfway up the wall, finding the handholds to scale it. He pulled himself up, his feet landing on the holds easily. He'd done this so many times by now, his brain had memorized the positioning of the things.

"That's it, Wonderboy!" Phil yelled as he scrambled higher and higher. "You're beating your top time!"

Hector's muscles tingled with excitement. He had almost reached the top when he saw the girl execute a parkourlike move over a hurdle, tucking her knees into her chest, then landing and rolling on the grass and popping back up on her feet.

What the . . . ?

"Good job, Mae!" her father called from the sidelines.

The move was graceful and elegant—completely captivating—and unlike anything Hector had ever seen. Not only that, but thanks to her fancy moves, she was gaining on him, even though she started well behind him on the course. How was that even possible?

Despite his attempts to focus and keep climbing, Hector couldn't take his eyes off her. He missed the next handhold by a mile and felt his other hand start to slip.

"Oh no," he gasped.

He made another grab for the handhold, but it was too late. His palms were slick with sweat, and the handles were too smooth. His stomach swooped as he fell backward off the wall.

"Noooooooo—" Phil yelled.

But there was nothing Hector could do. He plummeted toward the ground and landed on his back, hard.

Thud.

Pain flooded through his body while stars exploded in his vision. Breath gushed from his lungs from the impact.

Then everything went black.

4
TRIPPED AT THE FINISH LINE

Hector's eyes popped open. The sun glared down, making it impossible to see.

"Wh-where am I?" he stammered, feeling a rush of panic.

He was lying flat on his back on the soft grass of the field. He blinked and tried to focus. The last thing he remembered was climbing the wall, then watching the girl do that sick move, then losing his grip—and falling.

Oh no . . . I fell, he thought.

A familiar voice reached his ears. It sounded worried.

"Hector, you okay?" Phil said, patting Hector's shoulder. "If you are, then say something."

"*Something*," Hector managed weakly. His brother snorted a laugh. Hector flashed a wry smile.

"Well, if you can crack a joke, then you're probably not dying," Phil said, sounding more relieved than amused.

"Confirmed," Hector said. "Not dying, at least not yet. Can't get rid of me that easy."

"Thank the gods—all of them," Phil said. "But let's get you checked out to be safe," he went on. "Can you sit up?"

Hector did, but winced. His ribs felt bruised, though not broken, and his pride was damaged. But otherwise he felt okay. He looked up and caught sight of the girl and her father watching him.

Just great, Hector thought. Not only did she witness his embarrassing fall, but this new girl could actually beat him in the big race. She'd tackled the practice course like it was nothing.

Hector was sure that he was stronger and faster, but she was more nimble and graceful. She could probably climb more easily, and her efficient movements meant that she could catch up to him.

I could actually lose to her, he thought, anxiety coursing through him.

"So, if you're all right, do you want to tell me what happened there?" Phil said, helping Hector to his feet. "You got distracted, didn't you?"

"Yeah, I guess so," Hector admitted, glancing at the girl again. *Mae*. That was her name. He remembered her father calling her that. She was stretching on the sidelines, her father talking to her in low tones. Slowly, Hector dragged his gaze off her.

Why was she so distracting?

"When are you going to learn to focus?" Phil said, shaking his head in disappointment. "You could've gotten seriously hurt! You're just lucky you landed on a soft patch of grass. In the real races, you won't be so lucky. It'll be a mud trap . . . or worse."

Phil sounded upset—but also scared.

Hector looked down at the soft spot that had cushioned his landing. His brother was right. He was lucky. He could have seriously injured himself if he'd landed somewhere else. These races looked like fun, but they could be dangerous if the athletes weren't careful. This was just a practice course. The real race would have more obstacles designed to trip him up or even trap him.

Hector shuddered. His athletics career could end with one bad injury. He thought of his mother and the trophy case in their little shop. Winning the Cup wasn't just about bragging rights. It would help boost their business and also make his family proud. He couldn't fail them. He'd seen them get their hopes up with each of his brothers, then felt the dark cloud descend after they lost. He didn't want to see that same disappointed look in his mother's eyes after *his* race. Resolved, he decided to train harder and not get distracted ever again—especially not by Mae.

Phil helped him up, leading him over to a bench. He piled their bags on it.

"Wait here, I'll get the truck and pull around," Phil said, leaving Hector on the bench. "We'll get you checked out at the clinic to make sure you're okay."

Hector nodded, but he knew that he was. This wasn't his first fall. When he started training as a kid, he'd bit it more than once. But he appreciated that his brother cared and wanted to make sure he was all right.

While Phil pulled the truck around, Hector studied the practice course and its series of obstacles. The girl was breezing through them, twirling and tucking and leaping.

He couldn't stop watching her. The sun was just dipping into the horizon, casting a golden hue over the world. It was magic hour—the best time to take pictures because of the incredible lighting.

Hector snuck his camera from his bag and took some candid shots of Mae. Her ponytail whipped around her face as she ran. Her father trained her hard, coaching her from the side of the field.

Hector zoomed in, focusing on her face. Her brow was furrowed in deep concentration, her eyes were locked forward on the next obstacle, and her cheeks were flushed from the effort.

Snap. Snap. Snap.

Hector fired the camera, recording her image while the golden sunlight cascaded over the field. He zoomed in even closer on her face. Suddenly, she turned and looked right at him—their eyes locked through the camera viewfinder.

Hector quickly lowered the camera, but it was too late—she'd caught him taking her picture. He should've asked her permission first, he knew. He resolved to delete all the shots once he got home. How humiliating. Why did he keep watching the girl? Why was she so distracting?

Just a few seconds ago, he'd promised that he would focus and work harder. It was like she had some magic power to lure his attention. He couldn't explain it.

He hid his camera in the bag, zipping it up right as Phil pulled around. The truck chugged, spewing exhaust fumes. Hector's heart thumped harder.

That was close.

* * *

"Rise and shine, Wonderboy!" Phil called. "It's prelim time!"

Hector groaned in his bed, then sat up sleepily. He didn't feel like a Wonderboy. Even though he wasn't hurt from the fall, not really. The soreness in his ribs had already faded away, but he didn't feel up to the race at all. He turned and squinted at the window. At least it looked like a lovely, sunny day.

Hector sat up and grabbed his camera. He thumbed the buttons, navigating to the saved pictures and pulling them up on the digital screen. Mae's face flashed across it. They were zoomed-in close-ups. Her intensity was clear in her gaze.

Despite his promise to himself to delete them, he hadn't yet. He'd told himself that it was smart to study the competition. But really, he was fascinated by the way she ran the track. Something about her just captivated him. Maybe it was how she seemed so confident and sure of herself—the opposite of how he felt.

Who are you? he wondered, flipping through the images so fast they became animated and looked alive, like in a movie.

Still, he resolved that he wasn't going to lose to her, not today. He'd trained practically his whole life for this race. This was the final practice run before the real deal next week. Everyone in town would show up to watch.

He was ready.

He had to be ready. He didn't have a choice. Unlike taking pictures, where he could always take another one, or edit them to fix the mistakes, in racing there were no do-overs or repeats. You only got one chance to win the Zeus Cup.

With a sigh, he flicked his camera off and set it aside, then got busy changing and getting ready for the race.

"You ready for this?" Phil said when Hector appeared

in the kitchen in his racing uniform. It had lightning bolts across the chest.

"You know it!" Hector said, mustering up as much enthusiasm as he could.

"Good luck," his mother and father said in unison, making his mom chuckle.

"We'll meet you at the track with the rest of the entourage," Dad added with a wink.

"Dad, your brothers do *not* count as your entourage," Juan said.

"Yeah, plus you gotta be famous to have an entourage," Luca added.

"Wow, teenagers," Dad said with a snort. "Can't live with them . . . wait, that's it. That's the whole saying."

"Wish they'd told us what we signed up for at the hospital before we took you home," Mom added with a wicked grin. "Should've read the fine print."

They both laughed while Luca and Juan pouted. Hector shouldered his athletic bag and headed for the door behind Phil.

"Love you guys," he said, suppressing a grin at his family's antics. "See you at the track."

* * *

When the starting buzzer went off, Hector felt his heart vault into his chest like it was leaping over a hurdle. He clenched his jaw and bolted off the starting blocks. As he sucked in a breath and pumped his legs, he smelled a mix of fresh-cut grass, mud, and sweat—the familiar aroma of racing. A mix of local twelve-year-olds, of all genders, ran the practice course alongside him, including Mae. But Hector flat-out refused to even glance in her direction. He got off to a strong start, his legs propelling him forward toward the first obstacle—a series of hurdles. He leapt over them, feeling his heart thump, fast and steady.

Hector led the pack as they reached the more difficult obstacles, splashing through mud, climbing ropes, and vaulting walls. With each obstacle the course seemed to get harder and trickier, but he'd been training so hard he knew how to handle them. Practically the whole town had shown up to watch. They packed the stands and cheered for their kids or for their favorite. Hector could hear his name echoing over the course.

"Go, Hector!"

"Wonderboy, you've got it!"

Hector flew over the mud pit, swinging from one rope to the next like Tarzan. He heard his mother whoop and tried not to smile.

No distractions.

"Stay focused," Phil called out.

When Hector glanced over at him, he saw someone gaining on him from the corner of his eye. It was Mae. Of course it was. Hector looked ahead and refocused. It didn't matter where she was. Hector was determined to win.

His breath grew short. Sweat dripped down his brow, stinging his eyes.

His gaze locked onto the next obstacle—the highest and last wall.

He dug his shoes into the grass and leapt over the mud pit at its base, flinging his body at the wall ahead and starting to scramble up it. Down below, the mud pit glistened in the midday sun, thick and goopy, threatening to trap anyone unlucky enough to slip off and fall.

He climbed faster, but Mae was behind him, right on his heels.

Stay focused, he told himself, climbing higher. *Don't let her distract you*.

He reached the top. Over it, he could spot the finish line just ahead. All he had to do was make it over, climb down, then sprint through it.

But then he heard her voice. "Help!"

Hector glanced down and saw the distressed look on Mae's face as her feet slipped out from under her. She clung to the wall by only one hand, about to fall.

Hector remembered his fall at the field and how bad it hurt—how freaked he'd been after being knocked out. He knew he should focus on the race. She was his competitor—not his friend. He didn't have to help her. He could hear Phil yelling at him from the sidelines.

"Why are you stopping?! Stay focused! You're almost there!"

But Mae looked desperate. Her eyes were wide and full of fear.

"Please help me!" she whimpered.

Hector knew he should just keep climbing, but he couldn't let her fall. It wasn't the right thing to do.

He was better than that.

"Here, grab my hand," he said, reaching down to help her back onto the wall. She reached her free hand up.

But instead of letting him help her, she yanked him down, causing him to slip. He clung to a handhold with one hand. It all happened so fast. As he dangled there, she shot him a wicked smirk, then climbed up the wall and sprang onto the top of it.

She'd tricked him.

"What're you—" But Hector didn't finish the question, because his hand, which was slick with sweat, slipped from his handhold.

"Noooo!" Phil shouted.

Hector plummeted toward the giant mud pit. He tried to grab on to a handhold as he fell, but his fingers couldn't grasp it. Distantly, he heard cheering as Mae crossed the finish line.

Then he felt it—

Splash.

He was done for.

5
DAMSEL IN DISTRESS...*NOT*

Splash. *Splash. Splash.*

Hector scrambled to get out of the mud trap, slipping on the slick sides and sinking deeper into the muck. It clogged his mouth and nose, tasting horrible. He choked and gasped for breath.

He could hear Mae cheering her win on the other side of the wall.

Did she just play dirty to win? Hector thought as he frantically sloshed around in the thick mud, trying to wriggle out. It was harder than it looked. The mud trap was designed to keep racers . . . well . . . trapped. The other kids would catch up soon.

How could she do that to him? Sure, sabotage was

technically allowed in these races, but it wasn't considered good sportsmanship. Hector would never play dirty like that. Sure, his family wanted the Zeus Cup, but they wouldn't approve of him cheating.

"Hurry up, get out of there!" Phil yelled at him from the sidelines. His face was flushed and angry. "You've still got a chance to place!"

But other kids were racing past him, jumping over the mud pit and onto the climbing wall. Hector wanted to give up, but he heard his brother's voice. He couldn't quit now. He summoned the last of his strength.

Hector scrambled harder, finally wriggling his way out of the mud trap. But he was soaked and covered head to toe in muck. He probably looked like some kind of swamp creature. His favorite uniform was ruined.

Somehow, though slipping and sliding the whole way, Hector made it up the wall and down the other side. All he had to do now was sprint to the finish. His shoes squished with each step, oozing mud and making it impossible to run at his usual speed.

Squish-squish-squish went his shoes. *Thump-thump-thump* went his heart.

He was exhausted from his struggle and completely winded. Hector limped over the finish line, placing a distant tenth. He was filthy and soaking wet and out of breath. And beyond livid. This wasn't fair, not by a long shot.

How could she?

His eyes locked onto Mae as she accepted the blue ribbon for placing first in the preliminary race. It wasn't the Zeus Cup, thankfully, and they'd both qualified for the big race. But it still stung to lose, especially like that.

"You got distracted, didn't you?" Phil said, coming over with his clipboard. He slapped it on his leg in disappointment. "It's what I'm always warning you about in training. When are you going to learn to focus?"

"But she cheated!" Hector whined. "She tricked me to win."

"That's not an excuse," Phil said with a frown. "If you'd stayed focused on your own race and not worried about her, this wouldn't have happened. You should've listened to me."

"But it's not fair," Hector said in a petulant voice,

slumping down in defeat. He could taste mud on his tongue. It dripped down his face. Frustrated tears pricked his eyes.

"Hector, you need to take responsibility for your loss," Phil said. "That's the only way you're going to learn and improve before the big race. You can't blame the girl. It's your fault."

With one more pointed look, Phil left him alone to go talk to his parents in the stands. They watched him with gloomy expressions. He'd let them all down.

Hector limped over to his bag and pulled out a towel, trying to clean himself off. But all he could do was smear the mud around. He felt humiliated, but also furious. Despite what his brother said about taking responsibility, he still felt cheated. He was just trying to be nice, and he'd been punished for it.

Hector glanced up and spotted Mae off to the side of the track with her father, grinning and preening. The blue ribbon hung around her neck.

That ribbon should've been mine, Hector thought angrily.

He had been beating her fair and square before she

pulled that dirty trick on the wall. The only reason he lost was because she pretended to be a damsel in distress, even though she didn't actually need help. It was all a ruse, plain and simple.

And he fell for it like a fool.

Before he knew what he was doing, he started toward her to confront her about what she'd done. Anger propelled him across the field, shooting through his muscles like fire.

But then, Mae's father yanked the blue ribbon from her neck, crumpled it up, and threw it down on the ground.

"You don't deserve this," he barked at her, angrily tapping his clipboard. "You fell short of your top time. You're slacking off out there."

Hector stopped in his tracks, shocked.

Her dad was lecturing her? Even though she'd won?

Mae looked crestfallen. She scrambled to pick up the ribbon, crumpled and dirty as it was.

"I'm sorry, Papa," she said, looking down at her shoes in shame.

"You almost lost to that boy," her father went on.

"You're just lucky he got distracted. Next time, you won't be so fortunate. The big race is next week."

"I know," Mae said, blinking to hold back her tears. "I promise, I'll train harder in our backyard course."

"No, we're hitting the public track again," her father continued. "Clearly, you got distracted because you're not used to racing in front of other people."

So that explained why Hector hadn't seen her training before this week. She had her own private training course.

"Winning the Zeus Cup is important for your future," her father asserted. "Don't you want to win a track scholarship to college?"

As her father continued to lecture her about focusing harder on her training, Hector realized they had a lot more in common than he imagined. Now he understood why she pulled that dirty trick on the wall. She felt pressure from her family to win, just like he did.

Sure, he wouldn't have played dirty like that. But he understood why she did. Slowly his anger subsided and morphed into something else — sympathy.

He felt bad for her because he knew exactly what that

felt like. Making sure that nobody was watching, Hector pulled his camera out of his bag.

He aimed it at Mae and focused on her face as she swiped at her eyes, wiping sweat away. He zoomed in closer and focused the lens.

It wasn't sweat dripping down her cheeks. She was crying. He felt another surge of emotion as he studied her face.

Snap. Snap. Snap.

He captured a few quick pictures. Then he turned away to examine the images. The sun glinted in his eyes, distorting the screen. Suddenly, he felt someone grab his shoulder.

"Hey, what do you think you're doing?"

6
DREAMS ARE FOR ROOKIES

Hector looked up in surprise.

Mae.

She glanced at the camera clutched in his hands—and the candid photo of her face displayed on the screen. In the image, her lips were twisted into a frown. Tears streaked her cheeks, mixing with sweat.

"Hey, you keep taking my picture," Mae snapped. "Are you, like, trying to steal my soul or something? Pretty sure that only works on vampires."

Hector's cheeks burned. He fumbled for words, but his tongue felt thick in his mouth, and nothing came out. Partly, he wasn't used to talking to kids his own age who weren't his brothers. But also, something about Mae unnerved him. She was just so . . . confident.

She didn't seem afraid, or to suffer from self-doubt that ate away at her insides. Maybe he was the only one who ever felt that way.

"Well, news flash . . . I'm not a vampire," she said, staring at him accusingly. "Are you trying to cheat? Like, get intel on me or something?"

Hector felt his cheeks turn even hotter, if that was possible. He couldn't believe *she* was accusing *him* of cheating. He felt like his entire head was on fire.

"Uh, I guess . . . I like taking pictures," he confessed. "And well, maybe I saw something in you that felt . . . familiar. I don't know. I can delete them."

Mae crossed her arms defensively, then shot him a cocky smile.

"What do you mean *familiar*? We don't have anything in common. I'm a winner—and you're a loser. Simple as that. I beat you today. And I'm going to win the Zeus Cup next week, too."

Hector glanced at her father across the field, chatting up the race officials, then over at his brother talking to his family by the stands. He didn't want anyone to hear them.

DREAMS ARE FOR ROOKIES

"Listen, I get why you did it," he said in a low voice, meeting her eyes. She flinched, but he plowed forward anyway. "My brother is super hard on me, too. I know he means well, but . . . my family just wants me to win the Cup. Even though it's not really what I want."

Mae's lips twitched, then she softened slightly. She glanced at her face in the picture.

She looked miserable.

"Yeah, my dad's dream is for me to win," she confided quietly. "He wants me to get an athletic scholarship to college. He thinks the Zeus Cup is the ticket for recruiters to start noticing me."

"But is that really your dream?" Hector prodded. He stared at her for a long moment. The silence felt heavy.

Finally, Mae snorted.

"Dreams are for rookies."

Hector laughed. "Look, you can tell me the truth. What do you want?"

Mae hesitated, then finally spoke. "You're right, I hate racing. I love playing guitar and wanna join a band."

"Whoa, that's super cool," Hector said. "What kind of music do you like to play?"

"Punk," she said with a smirk, forming devil horns with her hand. "I like to rock out, what can I say?"

"Wow!" he said, surprised. "That's serious. I mean . . . I had no idea."

"Well, how would you know?" she pointed out. "You just met me. I haven't seen you around school at all."

"Right, I'm homeschooled along with my brothers," Hector said. "My dad teaches us. It means I can spend more time on my training. What about you? Haven't seen you at the field after school, either."

"That's cuz my dad set up a training course in our backyard at home," she said with a shrug. "Same idea . . . so I can focus on racing and not get distracted."

They both laughed together in commiseration. *Better to laugh than cry*, Hector decided in that moment.

They did have a lot in common.

"Well, I'd love to hear you play sometime," Hector said. "I love that kind of music."

"Not gonna happen," Mae said, her face sagging along with her shoulders. "My dad won't let me join a band."

"Why not?" Hector asked.

"He thinks my music just sounds like a bunch of

noise," she said sadly. "And that it won't help me get into a college, which is all he cares about. My mom is the same way."

"Yeah, that's how my family feels about my photography," Hector said, gesturing to his camera. He glanced over at his parents across the field. "They think it's a waste of time that won't help me win the Zeus Cup."

"Sounds familiar," Mae said, biting her lower lip.

"Wanna be friends?" Hector asked, holding out his hand. "What do you say? I could use a friend who isn't related to me."

That made her laugh. She stared at his hand, hesitating for a minute. "You're kind of covered in mud."

"Yeah, and whose fault is that?" he joked back.

Mae smiled. "Fine, we can be friends," she said, shaking his hand, mud and all. "But don't think this means I won't still beat you next week."

"I'd expect nothing less." Hector smirked. "Except you've got that wrong. Next week, *I'm* winning the Cup."

They shared a smile.

"Hector, let's go!" Phil called, glancing at Mae suspiciously and obliterating the moment. "Time to go home!"

Clearly, Phil didn't like that they were talking. Hector backed away, not wanting to leave Mae but not having a choice. When he climbed into the truck, Phil gave him a distrustful gaze.

"Look, you can't be getting distracted like that," Phil said. "What were you talking about anyway?"

"Uh, just racing and stuff," Hector mumbled, feeling flames tickle his cheeks again. "You know, she's actually pretty nice—"

But Phil cut him off.

"Listen, she's your top competition for the Cup. She bested you today—you can't be friends with her. Trusting her is the reason you lost the prelim."

Hector's stomach sank as they drove out of the parking lot. Phil was right. Mae had cheated him out of the win. But he saw something in her that reminded him of *himself*. Just like her, he often felt as if he didn't belong in his family. They never seemed to understand him or what he really wanted. He could sense that Mae was similar to him. She had a passion, and it wasn't racing or winning the Zeus Cup.

He glanced back at the field. She had returned to

her father's side. They were packing up to go home. She looked over at him in the truck and waved.

He lifted his hand to wave goodbye to her, but then caught sight of Phil's disapproving gaze and lowered it. His brother just wanted what was best for him, even if it wasn't what he himself wanted.

His eyes lingered on Mae anyway, until she vanished from the rearview mirror. Phil zipped into the town square and past the statue of Hades. Hector stared at the god. Suddenly, the statue's eyes glowed with yellow light. They tracked after him as the truck drove past, fixing on his face.

Hector flinched, but this time he didn't say anything to Phil, knowing his brother was already annoyed. When he glanced over again, Hades looked perfectly normal. Still, Hector couldn't shake the eerie feeling that he was being watched.

What was up with that statue?

* * *

Back at home, despite his mom and dad's attempts to appear cheerful at dinner—takeout pizza from his favorite local joint, Dionysus, named after the Greek god, of course—Hector could tell they were disappointed in his performance in the preliminary race. Even the pizza didn't cheer Hector up. He felt like a failure.

"Chin up, Wonderboy," Mom said, patting his shoulder and giving him another slice of pepperoni. "You'll show 'em at the real race."

"Tenth place isn't that bad," Luca offered. "I came in twelfth my year."

"Yeah, man," Juan added. "You're, like, way better than us. Not as good as Phil, though. He's the best."

"Until now," Phil said, getting up from his chair and kneading Hector's shoulders on his way to the refrigerator.

"Yeah, you'll bring the Zeus Cup home next week," Dad added with a wink. "We believe in you, son." He looked up at Phil as he returned to the table with a glass of water. "In both of you."

"Yup, today was an accident," Phil agreed, shoving pizza in his mouth and talking while chewing. "He was going to win. Wonderboy just got distracted."

Hector frowned. "Yeah, I'm sorry. I promise to focus. It won't happen again."

"Hector, we saw what happened on that track," Dad said, catching his mother's eye. "You did the right thing trying to help that other racer. Don't *ever* feel bad for being a good person."

Mom nodded sharply. "That's how we raised you. It's not your fault that some people don't play by the rules."

Hector smiled his thanks. The pizza hadn't made him feel better, but that did.

After dinner, he went to brush his teeth. His mood was slightly better. His thoughts drifted back to Mae on the field. She was his competition. Phil was right. But couldn't she be his friend, too?

I want a friend.

He and his brothers might have been close, but they were related to him. That meant they had to like him. They didn't exactly have a choice.

Mae was different, and he liked it. She didn't have to be his friend. In fact, she even had a good reason not to be his friend. But she'd shaken his hand and agreed. The thought of it made him smile. His mouth was foamy with toothpaste. He spat in the sink and switched the water on, watching it swirl around and run down the drain.

He sniffed, smelling the minty flavor, but also something else —

Was that . . . *smoke*?

He crinkled his nose. That was strange. The smell grew stronger.

Where was it coming from?

He was about to call out to his parents to make sure everything was okay in the kitchen when smoke started pouring out of the faucet, filling the bathroom. Hector coughed hard. It stung his eyes. He waved it away from his face, scrambling to shut off the tap and make it stop.

Then, suddenly, a blue flame flashed in the mirror. The same color he had seen in the park on the Hades statue.

Hector jumped back in alarm.

Two yellow eyes peered out at him from the depths of the mirror.

They stared deep into his eyes.

A voice echoed through the bathroom. Like a sleazy car salesman, but deeper and more frightening.

"Hey, Wonderboy! Yah wanna win that Zeus Cup, don't yah?"

7
WHERE THERE'S SMOKE...THERE'S FIRE

"**N**o, that's impossible. . . ."

Hector dropped his toothbrush and backed away from the blue flame. It continued flickering in the depths of the reflective glass, casting eerie sapphire shadows across the bathroom's walls.

The only answer was a creepy cackle echoing out of the mirror.

Hector held his breath. Now he wasn't just seeing strange things—he was hearing them, too.

"Wh-who are you?" Hector stammered, chills erupting all over his body. "Wh-what do you want?"

The blue flame drew closer, revealing the outline of a figure with spiky flaming hair. Hector blinked.

But the blue flame was gone.

The bathroom was quiet.

Almost too quiet.

Hector leaned closer to the mirror, searching for the blue flame. He leaned in closer . . . closer . . . closer—

Knock. Knock. Knock.

The sharp rapping on the door made Hector almost jump out of his skin.

"Hey, Wonderboy! Did you fall into the toilet or something?"

It was just Luca.

Hector relaxed slightly.

"Yeah, you're not the only one that has to . . . ya know . . . go," Juan added loudly.

"No, me first," Luca said. "I knocked on the door. I got dibs—"

Hector could hear the sounds of them shoving each other outside the door. He shook his head to clear it, then worked to steady his breathing.

It wasn't real—it couldn't be real.

Blue flames didn't just appear in a mirror, or on statues in the park. And mirrors couldn't talk, either. Clearly, his eyes and ears were playing tricks on him. It was just the stress of losing the preliminary race, with the real race for the Cup only a week away, he reassured himself.

Feeling slightly better, he unlocked the bathroom door, letting his brothers shove their way past him, and headed off to bed. He collapsed, tiredness settling over his whole body like an iron weight.

* * *

The next day, Phil trained Hector hard at the field. "Remember, it's your dream to win this race," he lectured, putting him through the practice course and becoming more agitated every time Hector fell short of his best times.

The pressure was clearly getting to them both.

"Dreams are for rookies," Hector muttered under his breath, repeating what Mae had said, as he tackled the next obstacle—a rope climb that made his arms ache and quiver by the time he got to the top. He leapt to the ground, then ran for the hurdles that came next.

But his foot clipped one, taking it down and making his shin throb.

What is wrong with me today?

His heart just wasn't in it. The loss in the preliminary race had affected him more than he realized. He hadn't slept well, either. He felt sluggish, not like his usual self.

The school bell rang, and a few minutes later Mae took the field. She gave him a shy wave, then started limbering up under her father's careful watch.

Almost as soon as she arrived, she tackled the field with a verve and grace that Hector had never witnessed before. If she'd been good in training last week, this week she was better. It was like she was peaking.

And at just the right time.

Unlike Hector, who was dragging in his training—and his times reflected it. Despite their budding friendship, she was definitely his stiffest competition for the Zeus Cup.

"Hey, don't get distracted!" Phil yelled, spotting him watching Mae.

"Sorry." Hector panted, trying to catch his breath. Phil came over to him, clutching his stopwatch and clipboard.

"Look, you can't be her friend, remember? We talked

about this. She's not trustworthy," Phil said, softening slightly. "Remember what happened in the preliminary race? She played dirty once—she could easily do it again to win."

"It's not her fault," Hector argued. "She's not like that really. She's just under a lot of pressure from her dad."

"I know what I saw," Phil said, remaining skeptical. He narrowed his eyes at Mae as she did a parkour move over the hurdles. "Plus, that girl could beat you—even if she doesn't cheat."

"Yeah, I know," Hector said, feeling nauseated. His brother was right.

"What's gotten into you today?" Phil asked. "Your times are all over the place."

"Uh, I'm just tired, I guess," Hector managed. "Maybe it's the stress getting to me. And, well . . ."

They both turned to watch Mae as she climbed the same rope that Hector had struggled on like it was nothing, then leapt down and aced the hurdles.

Phil patted Hector's shoulder and lowered his voice.

"You're a faster runner, and stronger than her," Phil said. "But she's lighter and nimbler. She can climb the obstacles faster. And she's willing to play dirty."

"Sheesh, tell me something I don't know," Hector said, feeling even worse.

"Look, Mom and Dad told me not to say anything," Phil said. "But the shop is struggling. We're doing everything we can to keep it afloat. But the new megamart one town over has taken a lot of our best customers. It's not as easy for small businesses these days."

Hector's face fell; Phil noticed it.

"You can beat her, Wonderboy. I know you can," Phil said. "But you have to stay focused, got it? And that means the two of you can't be friends."

Hector nodded, playing along like he agreed with his brother, but the truth was starting to sink in. His life really wasn't his own.

* * *

That night, Hector had a terrible nightmare where the shadows on his wall formed images of losing the Zeus Cup to Mae.

She raced past him, crossing the finish line to cheering crowds and applause.

The shadowy figures then showed Mae holding the

Zeus Cup, hoisting it over her head, while Hector looked on in defeat, his shoulders sagging.

The crowd lifted Mae onto their shoulders, parading her around.

"Noooooo!"

Hector woke up in a sweaty panic, gasping for breath. He was still in his bed. His heart thumped wildly.

"It was only a bad dream," he whispered to himself. "It wasn't real. You're just stressed out."

Then something moved in the corner of his vision. He snapped his head around to look at the wall. The shadow figures were still there.

No. That's not possible.

Before his eyes, the shadows transformed into two hideous monsters. They loomed over him. Their claws stretched out toward him.

They aimed their claws at his neck.

And then—

They cackled.

8
PAIN AND PANIC

"No . . . please . . . don't hurt me!" Hector stammered.

He stared at the fearsome creatures with their large yellow eyes, shadowy bodies, jagged teeth, and razor-sharp claws. Impossibly, they jumped down off the wall, landing on his mattress with a solid *thump* that shook the bed. The monsters were real.

He couldn't believe his eyes. Fear flooded through him, making his palms sweat and his mouth run dry at the same time. Hector scrambled backward in his bed, trying to get away from them. His eyes stayed fixed on the nightmarish demons.

One was short and plump with a round torso,

jagged teeth, and a forked tail, while the other was skinny and taller with a beaky nose and horns. They both had sharp claws.

They took a step toward him.

Hector tried to back up more, but he hit the headboard of his bed.

He was trapped.

His heart veered into overdrive, making him pant like he did when he ran sprints at the track. Only there was nowhere to run this time.

"Wake up!" Hector hissed, pinching his arm to jolt himself awake. "It's just a nightmare! They're not *real*—"

"Pain, is he talkin' to us?" the skinny one hissed to the fat one, sounding perplexed.

"Uh, should we talk back?" the fat one said in a raspy voice.

"Yeah, and who's he calling not *real*?" the skinny one added, sounding quite offended.

The demons could . . . talk?

Hector shut his eyes and squeezed them hard, expecting the monsters to vanish like the blue flame in the mirror when he looked back. But when he cracked his eyes open again, the demons were still there.

They stared right back at him.

Then they burst into laughter.

"Oh, he thought we'd disappear!" the skinny one said, elbowing the fat one. "Though that would be a neat trick."

"Yeah, maybe there's a potion for that," the other one said. "We should ask the Boss Man."

Somehow their laughter scared Hector even more.

"No! Don't hurt me!" He gulped, yanking the blanket up to his neck to try to protect himself, even though that was silly. What was a blanket going to do against demons with sharp claws? "Please leave me alone!" he said, scrambling back and bumping into the headboard again.

"Oh, hey there, Wonderboy—" the tall, skinny one started. He took a step closer on the bed and raised his claws toward Hector.

"Wait, how do you know my name?" Hector stammered.

"Just calm down, kiddo!" the fat one added. "Don't panic—"

"Hey, that's *my* name!" the tall one said in excitement.

He jumped up and down on the bed, making it shake again.

"Please, don't hurt me!" Hector whimpered, trying to hide under the blanket.

"Sorry, we didn't mean to scare yah," the skinny one said.

"Boss Man just told us—*Show Wonderboy what happens if he refuses to accept our help,*" the fat one added cheerfully. "So we did."

Hector looked back and forth between the two monsters, perplexed. That wasn't what he thought demons were supposed to sound like. They were chipper and upbeat, friendly even.

This is not good, Hector decided. *I am definitely losing it.*

"Wh-what do you want from me?" he forced out.

"There yah go! Now you're getting with the program!" the fat one said. "I'm Pain, and that's Panic." He jerked his thumb to the skinny one, who grinned with sharp teeth, though it looked more like a fearsome snarl.

"Our boss has some powers that could help you win the Cup," Panic chimed in.

They both leered at him, which did not come off as

friendly. Their eyes, Hector realized, weren't smiling. They looked cunning.

"Yah wanna win the Zeus Cup, right?" Panic said, luring him.

He held up his hands, and a shadowy Cup appeared in them. He held it up like a prize.

Hector swallowed hard against his fear. Their offer, however suspect, was tempting. He felt fear slosh around in his gut. He remembered training at the track today and watching Mae, and realizing that he could actually lose to her next week.

Suddenly, the shadow Cup vanished into thin air, just like Hector's dream of winning could.

"Wh-who's your boss?" Hector forced out. "What can he do to help me?"

"Uh, the Boss Man," Panic said, gesturing for Hector to follow him. "We'll take you to him."

"I dunno," Hector said, hesitating. "It sounds fishy."

"Wonderboy, you wanna win that Cup or not?" Pain rasped.

"Yeah," Panic said. "Otherwise . . . we can go talk to the girl—"

"Mae?" Hector blurted.

"Yeah, that's the one! I bet she wants to win bad enough that she'll listen to us. Why don't we just—"

"No." Hector cut them off. "I want to win!"

He couldn't let them talk to Mae. She'd take their help for sure, and then he'd *definitely* lose. He imagined how disappointed his family would be if he let that happen. No, not disappointed—devastated. He steadied his breathing and met their eyes, returning their stares.

"You can take me to your boss. I'll see what he has to offer."

* * *

Pain and Panic helped Hector sneak out of the house. It was still the middle of the night, and his family was sound asleep.

He crept down the shadowy hall, following Pain and Panic, who ended up tripping and stumbling over each other in their excited rush to get to the front door.

"Quiet!" Hector hissed at them as they landed in a heap on the floor. "Are you trying to wake up every single member of my family?"

Hector froze and listened closely. But he didn't hear anyone stir. His dad's snores still drifted through the thin walls.

He relaxed. Luckily, they were all deep sleepers. An elephant could've crashed through the front door, and his dad would have probably kept right on snoring.

Even better, his little bedroom was near the front door. He didn't have to go downstairs. He just had to cross the living room and make sure the door didn't creak on its hinges.

Pain and Panic crept ahead, leading the way and signaling when it was safe to follow. Their shadows cast across the walls by the hall light looked terrifying.

But they seemed so calm and friendly, although Hector suspected that was more of an act and that they could easily shift back into terrifying demons at the command of their Boss Man.

Whoever he was.

Hector felt a pang of fear prick his stomach. It probably wasn't smart to follow two strange demons in the middle of the night to meet their mysterious boss.

But then he remembered the nightmare they had enacted for him, where he lost the Zeus Cup to Mae. This might be his only chance to ensure that he won.

Plus, they'd threatened to talk to her if he didn't take the deal. She was clearly willing to play dirty to win. He couldn't risk it.

Hector continued after Pain and Panic, tiptoeing through the living room. He didn't breathe until they reached the front door and climbed down the front steps. Pain and Panic, in their joyous rush to be outside, tumbled over each other, landing in a pile of claws on his front lawn.

"I said, be quiet! My family might sleep like the dead, but my neighbors don't," Hector hissed at them. "And they'd probably find it suspicious to discover two demons lurking in the cul-de-sac."

Pain and Panic led Hector out of his neighborhood, down the street, and toward the center of town. It was such a small town that it didn't take long to get there on foot. Plus, Hector was in good shape. Jogging a few miles was nothing to him. He wasn't even winded.

"Where are we going?" he asked, surveying the deserted downtown area. Nothing stayed open this late around here.

Hero's Sporting Goods was all closed up with the doors locked. Through the windows, he could see the trophy case in the dimly lit interior.

"This way, Wonderboy," Pain and Panic said, cutting into the park in the middle of town—the one with the statues of the Greek gods in the center.

The demons led him right up to the statue of Hades. The white marble face with flaming hair and pointy teeth stared down at him. Being this close to it made Hector's knees shake. He couldn't forget how the statue's head had burst into blue flames the other day.

But his eyes had been playing tricks on him—or had they?

"You took me to . . . a statue?" Hector said, trying to sound more annoyed than scared.

"Just wait!" the demons said, hopping up and down.

They peered up at Hades excitedly.

"We're here, your most lugubriousness," Pain called up to the statue.

But nothing happened.

"This is a total waste of time," Hector said, feeling a touch relieved. He was just imagining things after all. "And now I'm going to be tired for training today—"

Suddenly, blue flames sparked, igniting the hair of the Hades statue.

Hector froze, his heart jumping into his throat. The flames licked the god's forehead—just like the vision Hector had the other day—and lit up the park with flickering light.

"Wh-what's happening?" Hector stammered, terrified.

With another burst of flames, the Hades statue came to life. Hades' eyes glowed fiercely yellow, staring down at Hector with obvious pleasure as he unfurled his marble arms and reached for him.

Then his voice echoed out from the statue, deep and smarmy. It reverberated through the empty park.

"Well, well, Wonderboy, I presume?" Hades said with a wicked grin. "You're a little late, you know. I don't like waiting."

9
SMALL UNDERWORLD
AFTER ALL

"Th-that's impossible," Hector sputtered, staring up at the giant statue that had just sprung to life. He couldn't believe his eyes. "How are you doing this?"

Even Pain and Panic lurked back in the shadows, clearly afraid. The statues of the other gods watched over them with placid expressions, still and silent.

"Hey, kid, Zeus isn't the only one who can pull this statue trick." Hades smirked. "Don't insult me."

Hector's eyes flicked to the Zeus statue. He ruled

over all the gods and Mt. Olympus, where they lived. But he wasn't coming to life at the moment. Hector couldn't believe what was happening right now.

He was talking to Hades.

"Zeus . . . as in your brother?" Hector said, his mind whirling.

Anger flashed in Hades' eyes. The blue flames on his head suddenly flared orange tinged with red, flaming hotter. Hector felt the heat surge, making his face burn.

"Ugh, my brother, yes," Hades said, rolling his eyes. "Don't remind me. Mr. High and Mighty, Mr. Hey, you! Get off of my cloud."

"Sorry," Hector said, backing up. "But what do you want with me? I'm just a kid—you're a god."

"Oh, right," Hades said in a casual voice. "You wanna win that Zeus Cup? Well, I can endow you with super-strength and speed—godlike powers—so you're a shoo-in to win." He leered down at Hector. "All you gotta do is drink this potion."

Hades snapped his fingers, summoning Pain and Panic.

"Coming, your most lugubriousness," Pain rasped

while Panic flicked his fingers, producing a crystal vial with a strange potion burbling inside.

They scrambled to approach the statue, tripping over each other in their haste.

"Careful," Hades snapped, flaming red again. "Those potions don't grow on trees."

Pain and Panic cowered back in fear. Hades turned to Hector, controlling his temper. His hair calmed into soft blue flames again.

"Wonderboy, what do ya say?" Hades spoke impatiently. "Hurry up, I don't have all day . . . or rather, all night. What time is it?"

Hector quickly thought it over, but something bothered him. He remembered the lesson on the Greek gods his father had taught.

"I'd say it sounds too good to be true," Hector said suspiciously. He stared up at Hades and crossed his arms. "What do you want from me? You must have a reason for doing this. You're Hades, after all."

"Ah, my reputation precedes me," Hades said with a knowing cock of his head. "All I ask in return is that you bring me the Zeus Cup after you win the race."

That seemed simple enough. Hector just wanted to win. He didn't actually care that much about the Zeus Cup itself. He could turn it over after he claimed the top spot in the race, right?

Then he remembered the empty trophy case in the store. His family was dying to display the Zeus Cup for the entire town to see.

"What do you want the Cup for? If I give it to you, will I eventually get it back?"

Hades smirked. "Of course, kid. If it means that much to you. As for what I want it for, I'm not sure I trust you enough to tell you. You gotta be careful who you tell secrets to, ya know?"

Hector hesitated. "Listen, it sounds really great, but if I'm going to win the Cup, I want to do it on my own merits."

"Ugh, so heroic," Hades said with annoyance. "You remind me of that other hero guy."

Hector had no clue who he was talking about, but didn't ask.

"Listen, kid, that girl you're up against? She already played dirty to win, remember?"

"Yeah, but that doesn't mean I should," Hector said, even as doubt seeped into his heart.

Making it worse, Pain and Panic morphed back into shadows, reenacting the scene from the preliminary race. He watched as Mae pulled him off the wall and into the mud trap.

Splash.

Wow. Had it really looked that bad? Hector felt humiliation surge through him like red-hot fire, just as searing as it was the day he lost to her. The same thing could happen again at the big race.

Hades sensed his opening. "Hey, if you don't want the deal, no biggie," he said shrewdly. "I can always take it to the girl—"

"No, don't do that," Hector said right away.

"So we have a deal?" Hades prodded, leering at Hector.

"Just tell me one thing," Hector said, stalling. His mind reeled as he thought it through. "Why do you want the Zeus Cup so bad?"

"Fine." Hades rolled his yellow eyes. "The Cup is the key to releasing me from the Underworld. My annoying older brother imprisoned me down here," he added, cocking a thumb toward the Zeus statue. "And well, kiddo, it's a small Underworld, after all. I'd like to get out, stretch my legs, breathe the fresh air for a change."

Hector knew that older brothers could be pretty annoying. But still, he hesitated, unsure if he could trust Hades. He was the God of the Underworld, after all.

"But what are you gonna do when you get out?" Hector asked, still suspicious. "Why now? Sounds like you've been locked up down there for a long time."

Hades' hair flashed orangey red again, but then he controlled himself, breaking into a charming smile. "Don't worry about it, kiddo. It's just some god stuff," he added with a wink. "The usual Mt. Olympus family drama. It doesn't concern mortals. So what do ya say? We help each other get what we most want? Or should I talk to the girl?"

Hades raised his eyebrows while Panic held up the potion vial, tempting Hector with it.

He thought the deal over. He couldn't stand to lose again. His whole family was counting on him. Plus, if he didn't take the deal, then Mae would definitely accept it. All the training he'd done for the last two years would be for nothing. The thought made him feel sick.

Hades was right. Mae had been willing to play dirty to win.

Why shouldn't he do the same thing? It was just a little help. And no one would ever know.

"Fine, I'll do it," Hector said at last. "I'll drink the potion."

Really, he didn't have a choice. This was the only way he could ensure that he'd win the race.

"As you wish," Hades said, gesturing to Panic.

Before he could second-guess himself, Hector snatched the potion from Panic's hands. He removed the stopper, took a deep breath, then drank it down in one gulp. The liquid tasted bitter and foul, almost like rotten eggs, and it singed his tongue and throat.

Then, suddenly, searing, burning pain shot through his entire body. His muscles cramped and bulged, rippling and feeling like they were tearing apart.

"Nooooooo!" Hector screamed, writhing in pain and falling to the ground. "What did you do to me?"

He flailed around on the ground, his whole body

burning. Stars danced in his vision. He was starting to black out from pain.

What did I just do?

Hades' cruel laughter filled his ears. "Sorry, I forgot to mention that getting superstrength and speed might hurt just a little bit."

A little bit? Hector thought. He was in the worst pain of his life, worse than when he fell off the wall in practice and lost consciousness, worse than when Mae pulled him into the mud trap. His body twisted and contorted while his muscles bulged out and rippled.

He tried to cry out again, but no words escaped his lips.

Then his vision went dark.

10
GO THE DISTANCE

"**N**ooooooooo . . . I take it all back . . ." Hector gasped, waking up in a blind panic. He thrashed around in pain. "I shouldn't have drunk that potion!"

Searing pain still rippled through his muscles, though it began to fade as his eyes adjusted. He looked down. His body was twisted in his damp sheets.

He blinked in surprise—he was back in his little bedroom.

Not the town square.

How did I get back here?

He searched his memory and glanced around. Pale

dawn light streamed through the curtains. It was early morning.

Not the middle of the night.

It must've just been a terrible nightmare.

But it had all felt so real. The demons casting shadows on his wall and talking to him. The Hades statue catching fire and coming to life. Making that deal with the God of the Underworld for the Zeus Cup, then drinking that nasty potion.

Usually, he didn't remember his dreams. But that one was vivid in his mind like it had actually happened. He took a deep breath, then another. His pulse began to slow.

Demons weren't real. And even if they were, they certainly didn't talk like the ones he'd met. Also, statues couldn't catch on fire and come to life, or give you godlike powers. That meant one thing.

None of it was real.

Hector relaxed, the pain fading away completely. He flexed his muscles, expecting to wince.

But he actually felt . . . pretty good. Especially considering he clearly had a night fraught with fear. He decided he must be stressed about the upcoming race. Even that thought sent waves of anxiety running through him.

"Hector, get up for school!" his mother called, her voice echoing in from the kitchen.

"I'm up!" he called back. "Chill out," he added quietly, feeling annoyed.

He never got a day off. His weekdays were filled with homeschooling *and* training, then weekends were just entire days of training, or worse—race days.

Hector glanced at the calendar in his phone, even though he already had it committed to memory. The appointment stared right back at him—*Mt. Olympus Spartan Run.*

It was this Saturday, in two *short* days. He shut his phone, then glanced mournfully at his camera bag slumped on his desk. All he wanted was to take pictures and spend a whole day to himself, wandering around without a strict schedule and someone yelling at him to focus.

But it wasn't going to happen.

Still groggy, Hector climbed out of bed. But something

felt different. His body moved fluidly, effortlessly. He felt the taut strength flowing through his limbs. He peered down at his body—then reeled back in shock.

His arms rippled with fresh layers of lean muscle.

He tore off his shirt and studied his reflection in the mirror. What he saw in his reflection was . . . not possible. He looked as if he'd grown stronger overnight. He flexed his biceps, amazed at how strong and supple they felt. Next, he tried his calves and hamstrings with the same results. They looked and felt stronger, too.

Hector grinned at his reflection. Until understanding hit him. This *wasn't* possible. Which meant . . .

His nightmare hadn't been a nightmare at all.

Hector felt a chill remembering the blue flames exploding from the statue. It had actually happened.

But no. It couldn't have. These new muscles were just a result of his hard training. His efforts were finally paying off, and right on time for the big race.

His brother was a talented coach. And he'd been eating a ton of protein. That was all. Hector stared at his reflection, flexing again and feeling the power in his body.

He felt more confident than ever. The self-doubt that usually stayed curled in his gut also seemed to have vanished overnight.

Now that he thought about it, he did feel kind of like a god. He grinned at his reflection again. This was just what he needed to win the race and bring home the Zeus Cup.

I can't wait to race! he thought, maybe for the first time ever.

* * *

Hector felt confident stepping onto the field. He searched his mind for any glimmer of his usual self-doubt but didn't feel any of it, even though it was crunch time. Just two days before the big race.

"Excited to train today?" Phil said with a wink. Even he noticed the change in Hector's demeanor.

"You betcha," Hector replied, returning the wink with a cocky smile of his own.

He stretched to limber up—but really it was just for show. His body already felt loose and smooth as butter. He sauntered up to the start line of the practice course, crouched down, and waited for Phil's signal. His heart beat calmly, not even a bit on edge. That also was out of the ordinary.

Woot.

Phil blew his whistle and hit his stopwatch in sync. Hector took off like the wind was carrying him. He effortlessly blew through the first few obstacles. Usually that rope climb got him breathing hard, but not today. When he dropped down to the ground again, he glanced at his hands and feet in amazement. He wasn't the slightest bit winded.

"Keep it up!" Phil shouted.

Hector gritted his teeth and turned on the speed. He practically flew toward the climbing wall ahead. He scaled it, flipped over the top in a somersault, then landed on the other side in a graceful crouch.

How did I just do that? he thought.

But he didn't have time to waste marveling at his abilities.

He sprang up and booked it for the finish line, sprinting down the field. He blew through it as Phil clicked STOP on the stopwatch.

Phil glanced down, his jaw dropping. He scratched his head, rechecked the time, then checked it again. "I just don't understand it . . ." he muttered under his breath as he jotted it down on the clipboard where he recorded all of Hector's race times.

"Uh, what's wrong?" Hector said, watching his brother's confusion. "Did the stopwatch quit working or something?"

"No . . . it's working fine," Phil managed to get out. "Just . . . wow! Dude, you beat your best time!"

"Oh, I did?" Hector said, trying to act casual about it. "Awesome."

"Not just awesome! Amazing! Incredible! Wondrous!" Phil said. "You definitely earned your nickname today, Wonderboy."

"Thanks," Hector said with a smile. "I sort of feel like a superhero today." This all felt like a dream. He pinched his arm to make sure it was real life.

While Phil compared the times and made some calculations, Hector glanced across the field. Mae had arrived and was busy warming up.

Even she shot him an impressed look. His performance

had caught her attention. Their gazes met, but then she furrowed her brow and narrowed her eyes.

He studied her expression, trying to decipher it. It was . . . worry.

She was worried she could lose to him. It was the first time he'd seen her look anything but confident about beating him.

Phil clapped his shoulder, drawing his attention back.

"You beat it by a full thirty seconds!" Phil told him, looking up from his clipboard and shaking his head in disbelief. "Bro, how'd you get so much faster overnight?"

Hector just shrugged, trying to hide a sly smile. "It must be your coaching! How else do you explain it? Plus, my hard work. It's all starting to pay off."

He glanced back at Mae, but she'd returned to focusing on her own training. She didn't look back at him again. She might have been his friend—but she was also his competition. He couldn't treat her any differently from any other racer on that field.

I'm going to win that race, Hector decided. *Nothing can stop me now.*

He went to the public bathroom at the track. It was

empty and smelled like mildew despite the undercurrent of chlorine and bleach clinging to the air. The smell was comforting, however, in its total familiarity.

He washed his hands, then stared in the mirror at his new physique. He left the water running. It was just a weird dream. No way Hades was real.

"It's just my training," he repeated to his reflection. "That's why I'm faster and stronger—"

Suddenly, black smoke filled the air, gushing out of the water taps.

Hector coughed hard, then struggled to shut off the taps. His cheek brushed the mirror. His eyes burned from the sulfurous fumes.

Flash.

A blue flame ignited, dancing in the mirror. Two yellow eyes glinted out of the depths, boring into him. There was a sudden flash of Hector holding up the Zeus Cup in celebration, but then it erupted into flames.

Hector leapt back in fear, his heart practically exploding in his chest as a familiar voice echoed out of the mirror.

"Don't get cocky, Wonderboy! Remember our deal! Win the race—and bring me the Zeus Cup!"

11
ZERO TO HERO, JUST LIKE THAT

Hector backed away from the mirror in fear . . . *Hades was real!*

He did make the deal with the God of the Underworld. It wasn't just a nightmare. The amazing practice he'd just had, the thirty seconds he'd shaved off his time—it was all because of Hades and that awful potion.

And the god's message was clear—*What was given could be taken away.*

The blue flames turned red, erupting out of the mirror and singeing his face, while toxic smoke kept flooding the bathroom, choking him and stinging his eyes.

Hector coughed and sprinted for the door, when suddenly—

Bang. Bang. Bang.

Someone knocked on the door, making him jump back.

A familiar voice called out.

"Did you fall in or something?" Phil yelled, sounding impatient. "You still have to train. Hurry it up, daylight is wasting—"

Hector burst through the door, gasping for breath. The fresh air hit his lungs. He bent over, gulping it down like water.

Phil shot him a weird look. "Uh, I was totally kidding about the falling-in part. You okay?"

"Don't you see the fire?" Hector rasped.

Why wasn't Phil freaking out?

Phil held the bathroom door open and peered inside. Hector edged up behind him timidly. But the bathroom looked perfectly normal.

No flames.

No smoke.

No sign of Hades.

Nothing.

But it had all felt so real. He was sure about what he'd seen in there—what he'd felt and heard. Regardless, Hector couldn't let anyone know about the deal he made with Hades to win the Cup.

"Uh, I'm fine," Hector said, trying to catch his breath. "Just did some extra squats in the bathroom in front of the mirror, and I think the smell in there got to me."

"That's the attitude!" Phil said, clapping Hector's shoulder. "I knew you'd learn how to focus. But I'm sorry about the smell," he added, scrunching his nose.

Hector took a deep breath to steady his nerves, then followed Phil, passing by Mae on the way back to the field. He still felt rattled from his encounter with Hades.

She caught his eye. "Hey, what's gotten into you?"

Hector shrugged, trying to act nonchalant. He couldn't let her know that he'd made a deal with a god to win the race. Not that she'd even believe it was true. She'd probably just think he was going crazy.

"Just nervous . . . about the race, I guess," Hector mumbled.

She studied him for a long beat, not exactly buying it.

But then she shrugged it off. "Aren't we all? My dad is all over my case about it. May the best hero win out there."

She held out her hand to shake on it. He grasped her fingers, feeling the warmth of her strong, steady grip.

Their eyes met. They shared a moment of mutual respect—the bond of their friendship sealed in their handshake, which made Hector feel even guiltier about making the deal with Hades to help him beat her.

But what choice did he have? Besides, someone had to win.

He remembered Hades' warning in the mirror. The flames exploding and singeing his face. The black smoke choking his lungs. What would happen if he actually made the god angry?

He didn't want to find out.

* * *

Two days later, Hector lined up for the race. This was the biggest moment of his life. Everything was riding on what happened over the next few minutes. But as he got into starting position, he didn't feel nervous. He just wanted to get this over with, win the race, and get on with his life.

ZERO TO HERO, JUST LIKE THAT

He looked over at Mae, but she was focused on the course ahead, her jaw clenched in determination. Hector almost felt badly for her. She had no idea that she had no chance today.

Beep!

The starting buzzer went off—Hector shot off the starting block like he had wings on his heels. He'd never felt this strong and swift before. It was almost like he was riding a magical Pegasus.

Mae broke behind him in a tight second place, but Hector quickly outpaced her and widened his early lead. The other kids fell in a pack behind them.

"Go, Wonderboy!" His family cheered from the stands. Mom and Dad waved wildly. Even Juan and Luca were getting along and not squabbling for once.

Phil watched him excitedly from the sidelines, clutching his clipboard and stopwatch.

"You've got this!" he called out. "Just stay focused!"

Hector flew through the first few obstacles easily. Sure, he'd been fast and strong before, but this was completely different. It didn't even feel like he was trying hard, nor did he break a sweat.

This isn't racing, Hector decided as he ran even faster, *this is flying.*

Was this what it felt like to be a god? He remembered Hades saying that drinking the potion would give him godlike powers. *Wow, I never wanna go back to being mortal*, Hector decided. This was way better. It was effortless.

Mae never stood a chance. Hector's lead grew bigger and bigger with each stride of his strong legs. He reached the final obstacle—the big wall with the treacherous mud trap underneath it. This was where she'd tricked him in the preliminary race, but not this time.

Hector leapt onto it, flying over the mud trap, and scrambled up the wall lightning fast. Then he flipped over the top and landed in a graceful crouch. He sprang right back up.

The crowd went wild. Now they'd all taken up the chant.

"Go, Wonderboy! Go, Wonderboy! Go, Wonderboy!"

Hector sailed through the finish line to thunderous applause, but he didn't stop there. He kept sprinting toward the stands and ran straight into his family's waiting arms for a big group hug.

Juan and Luca hoisted him onto their shoulders, parading him around. He watched Mae cross the finish line in a distant second place. Her father kicked the turf in anger, while she looked bewildered. She shot Hector an accusatory look.

He felt a stab of guilt. He could tell what she was thinking.

How did he get that much faster overnight and beat me so badly?

He quickly looked away. She'd played dirty to win. Now it was his turn. It was what she deserved. So why did he feel so guilty?

He tried to shake the thought and focus on the cheering crowd. His family was so proud of him. He felt his guilt wash away and vanish in the shower of applause and praise.

"Hector, we're so proud of you!" Dad said, beaming. "You won the Zeus Cup! I always knew you'd win! Never had a doubt!"

"That's my Wonderboy," Mom said, hugging Hector fiercely. "Your grandparents, rest their souls, would be so proud of you for bringing the Zeus Cup home to our little family store."

"Mom . . . Dad . . . I love you," Hector said, hugging them back.

He had never felt so loved and adored as he did in this exact moment. It washed through him, making him feel golden and strong. That's when he knew that he'd made the right decision.

All the hard training was part of it, of course, but the deal with Hades had sealed his victory. One thought shot through his head.

It was worth it even if I had to play dirty to win.

Phil presented the glimmering, golden trophy to Hector with a tear in his eye. It was over two feet tall. The golden figure on top depicted Zeus holding a lightning bolt, ruling over Mt. Olympus.

"You did it, Wonderboy," Phil said, choking up. "You won, just like we always dreamed!"

He tried to pass the Zeus Cup to Hector, but Hector

made Phil hold it up with him. The trophy felt solid and strong in their shared grip.

"No, *we* did it," Hector said to Phil. "You were there every step of the way. I couldn't have done it without you. This is your trophy, too." He turned to his family. "All of yours!"

The Gomez clan all held the trophy up together as the crowd cheered them on.

12
WONDERBOY

"**H**ey, Wonderboy!" called a dad with his son, waving to Hector from across the street and summoning him over. "Please, can we take a selfie with you?"

Hector hesitated—he was already running late. He was carrying the Zeus Cup with him, so it was no wonder they recognized him. Only one short day had passed since he won the race, but it felt like the blink of an eye. He'd been walking around as if on a pink cloud. And now he had to be at Hero's to place the Zeus Cup in the trophy case and sign autographs to promote the store.

He had wanted to bring the Cup straight to Hades last night—let the god use it and give it back—but his family had thrown him a huge party, and he hadn't found a chance to leave. Now he was stuck. His parents expected the Cup to be displayed today. He just hoped he'd be able to sneak to the store later and grab it so he could bring it to Hades. Hector wasn't sure what Hades might do to him if he didn't make good on his half of their deal.

"C'mon . . . please!" begged the kid, who looked to be about five years old, with a messy head of bright red, curly hair. He peered at Hector with big, wide eyes.

The kid was starstruck.

Hector was running late, but he couldn't refuse.

"Uh, sure," he said awkwardly, posing with the man and his kid while hoisting up the trophy.

Click.

"Wow, this is so cool," said the kid, marveling at the selfie on his dad's phone. "I can't believe I got a pic with the champ! One day I wanna be a true hero like you."

He gazed up at Hector in awe while his dad looked on excitedly.

"Thanks for inspiring my kid," the dad said. "All he was doing was playing video games. But now he wants to join the track team."

"That's great!" Hector said, looking down. "You've just gotta work really hard, like me . . ." He trailed off, feeling like a total fraud. His stomach sank.

His hard work had not paid off. He'd only won because of Hades.

But he pushed that thought away. He had also worked hard. He had trained on that field every day for over a year. He deserved to win the trophy. The only reason he'd lost the preliminary race was because Mae played dirty. He could have won fair and square—he was sure of it.

"Nice to meet you," Hector muttered. He was still running late, so he hurried off, dodging more people calling out his name. Hector wasn't used to being recognized on the street, let alone asked for selfies like this, even if it was just in his small-town square.

But that's how it was now. Everywhere Hector went in Mt. Olympus, people cheered and called out *Wonderboy!* or they wanted selfies or autographs. He couldn't get one block down the street without getting a request.

Hector hurried toward Hero's Sporting Goods, hoping he wouldn't get stopped again. A long line snaked down the front of the store. The customers cheered for him when he walked into the shop. He gave them a sheep-ish wave and quickly ducked inside.

The bell let out a welcoming *jangle* as he rushed through the door, inhaling the familiar musty scents of leather and rubber.

Mom spotted him and rushed over from behind the register.

"You're late," she said, glancing at the clock impa-tiently. "What took so long? You're the fastest kid in this whole town."

Hector blushed. "Uh, I guess . . . my fans . . . kept stopping me."

"Already bragging about your entourage?" Phil teased, joining them. "Don't get a big head. You're still my littlest bro, remember?"

"Yeah, littlest," Luca added, skipping over with a goofy grin.

"Thank the gods I'm not the littlest anymore," Juan added in a low voice. "It was pretty rough before you were born."

All the brothers chuckled, just like old times, bring-ing Hector back down to Earth a little bit. It felt like he'd been floating on a cloud with the gods in Mt. Olympus ever since he'd won the race.

"Hey, now, let your brother enjoy it," Mom said, giving Phil a friendly squeeze. "He worked so hard. This is his moment to shine."

She led Hector across the store. He still clutched the Zeus Cup, carefully cradling it in his arms.

"Care to do the honors?" Mom said, producing a golden key and unlocking the trophy case. The glass door swung open, revealing the rich velvet-lined interior. His brothers all looked on. Hector could feel the weight of the Zeus Cup in his strong hands.

Dad came out from the storage room, whistling cheerfully and carrying a box of T-shirts.

"Look, the new shirts came in!" he said excitedly. His eyes landed on Hector. "Oh, is it time?"

Mom nodded. "Can't keep his fans waiting forever." Her eyes shifted to Hector. "You ready?"

She gestured to the trophy case. But Hector hesitated, still gripping the trophy. His hands felt sweaty. They all noticed his hesitation.

"Son, go ahead," Dad urged, setting the box down and

swiping a tear from his eye. "You earned this! We're so proud of you."

Dad held up his phone to document the moment.

"And so grateful," Mom added, giving him a proud smile. "We've never sold so much merchandise in just one day!"

"And these new T-shirts," Dad said, holding one up for Hector's inspection. "They'll fly off the shelves."

The shirts were bright crimson with a gold graphic of Hector holding the Zeus Cup. "Wonderboy" was emblazoned across the front in gold lettering. The back read:

Hero's Sporting Goods
Home of the Famous Zeus Cup

Both his parents stood waiting for him, but still he couldn't do it. He couldn't put the trophy in the case. He'd made a deal with Hades. What was he going to do?

His parents exchanged a look.

"Well, Wonderboy," Dad said. "What're you waiting for?"

"Yeah, you need me to coach you through this one, too?" Phil added, chuckling with Dad.

Dad Jokes forever.

But Hector couldn't even crack a smile this time. Reluctantly, he approached the trophy case that his family had specially constructed to house the Zeus Cup, hoping that one day one of their kids would finally win it and bring it home to their shop.

But his feet felt like lead weights were strapped to them. He tried to put on a brave face, but doubt ate away at him anyway. Hades' voice from the bathroom echoed through his head.

Remember our deal! Win the race—and bring me the Zeus Cup!

What if it was already too late? What if Hades was already angry that Hector hadn't yet brought him the Cup? Maybe he should just turn and run, bringing the trophy with him over to the park in the town square. But then he looked at his family's faces—they were all so proud, even Luca and Juan, who usually razzed him.

"Look, it's not like it's going anywhere," Mom said, patting the trophy case. "I know you're attached to it, but you don't have to worry. It'll be right here, safe and secure."

She dangled the golden key in front of him for extra emphasis.

"Yeah, you can visit it whenever you want," Dad added with a big grin. "I know I would."

Hector's eyes fixed on the golden key, then shifted to the trophy case made of glass. But that was exactly the problem. It would be too safe and secure. Locking the Zeus Cup inside the trophy case meant that it would be even more difficult to deliver it to Hades like he'd promised.

But then another thought shot through his head, loud and clear and powerful.

Maybe I should keep the Zeus Cup for myself?

For one thing, Hector didn't exactly need Hades anymore. He had already won the race, right? Plus, now that he considered it, how much had Hades really helped him? Hector had trained his whole life for that race.

Also, although he hated to admit it, Hector had never had it this good. Everyone in town loved him and thought he was a hero. Overnight, he'd become a local celebrity.

Kids were posting to social media, idolizing him. The local paper had even run a front-page story on him that morning, featuring a picture of him holding up the Zeus Cup at the top of the podium.

Hector glanced behind the register, where his mother had already framed the paper's front page. Mae stood below him in second place, wearing a tight smile.

Despite her frustration at losing, Mae had asked for his number after the race so that they could text and stay in touch. He could tell she was impressed by his athletic prowess. Heck, everyone was.

His eyes darted to the line waiting patiently outside the door for his autograph-signing session. His mother had pulled it together fast, hoping to bring some business into the store. If each of those people bought one shirt today, it would be a huge day for their bottom line.

Maybe it was a bad idea to free Hades from the Underworld, anyway. Zeus had probably locked him up down there for a good reason.

Hector took a deep breath, then came to a decision. He approached the trophy case and set the Zeus Cup inside, carefully nestling it on the red velvet shelving. The lights hit the trophy, making it glow with golden light. Dad snapped pictures while the rest of the family clapped for Hector.

Applause erupted from the folks outside the doors as Phil flung them open to the crowd.

With that, Mom shut the case and twisted the lock, securing it. Hector heard the lock click solidly into place and knew it was done.

He was keeping the trophy.

"Ready?" Mom asked, leading him over to a table draped with a white tablecloth. She pulled out the chair for him. A stack of glossy pictures of Hector holding the Zeus Cup waited next to a big pile of golden metallic Sharpies.

"Uh, guess so," Hector said, trying to put on a brave face for his family. "Here goes nothing."

But inside, his nerves flared. He glanced at the trophy case, where the Zeus Cup gleamed under the lights. A shudder of regret rippled through him, but he didn't have a choice now that the Cup was locked up. Unless he wanted to steal the key from his mother, a thought that made him shudder even more.

I won that race, he told himself. *I earned that trophy. I trained hard. I don't need Hades anymore.* He signed autographs with his nickname, *Wonderboy*, until the line dwindled, the stack of photos diminished, and his hand ached from the repeated motion.

"Hey, can I get a bottle of water?" Hector called to Phil, who was busy manning the register. When his brother didn't respond right away, he added in a snippy voice, "Like, now?"

"Yes, your highness," Phil said, rolling his eyes. "Just a little busy here."

"Well, you're only busy because of me," Hector said, feeling a surge of annoyance.

"And you only won because I coached you—" Phil shot back.

Before their argument could escalate, Mom popped over and set a bottle of cold water in front of Hector. She rubbed his shoulders while he slurped it.

"Wonderboy's just tired," she said in a kind voice. "He's been working so hard. Go easy on him, okay?"

But Phil shot Hector another disapproving look. "Like the rest of us haven't?" he muttered under his breath. "And he's getting the star treatment. Must be so hard on him."

Tension rippled between the brothers, but Hector ignored it and went back to signing.

Finally, after another hour, the line ended and Hector was off duty. He helped his family close up the shop for the day. When they turned out the lights, the Zeus Cup remained illuminated in the case. Light danced over its luminous surface, making it look alive.

I did that, Hector thought. *I'm the one who finally brought home the Zeus Cup.*

"C'mon, son, let's go home," Mom said, steering Hector out of the store. "You've worked hard enough, and we're so grateful."

Phil watched, locking the door behind them, while Hector sauntered down the sidewalk like he was walking on air.

* * *

That night, Dad cooked a celebratory dinner—carne asada tacos from an old family recipe. He'd been marinating the steak all day. After dinner, his family presented Hector with a special cake in the shape of the Zeus Cup.

Hector beamed. "Wow, thanks, everyone," he said.

"But the party last night was enough. You guys didn't have to do this."

"We wanted to," his mom said, kissing the top of his head.

After they polished off the vanilla buttercream cake, with Juan and Luca fighting over the last piece and Phil poaching it while they were busy squabbling, Hector offered to help clear the table and wash the dishes.

"No way!" Dad said. "You've worked hard enough. We've got this. You take some time off."

Hector retreated to his bedroom and shot Mae a text:

What's up?

They had texted some that morning, too, but just *good morning* and stuff like that. She had asked how his party was but hadn't said what her family had done last night. Little dots popped up to indicate she was replying.

So, wonderboy, how's it feel to be a true hero?

Hector hesitated, then wrote:

Honestly, it's pretty amazing! My family keeps stuffing me silly. I signed autographs today.

He stopped writing, feeling guilty. Mae wrote back.

Must be great. My parents are on me to focus and train harder. It feels like no matter what, i'm never good enough

Hector's stomach sank. He knew exactly how she felt.

I'm sorry. Wanna hang soon? I'd love to hear you play guitar.

He added a cute guitar emoji for good measure, then a devil's horns rock-on hand symbol.

If i can steal you away from your fans. Seems like you're going to be busy. Sure your schedule can handle it?

She sent a laughing face emoji and music notes. He laughed and replied:

Will make it happen.

With that, Hector shut his phone and opened his closet to get ready for bed. His whole body felt heavy and exhausted from the event today. A complicated mixture of thoughts whirred through his head as he pulled out his pajamas.

He still felt bad for beating Mae, but he had to shove that aside. Someone had to win and someone had to lose. Besides, she hadn't felt badly when she played dirty to beat him in the preliminary race. It was time to move on. And Mae did win second place, which was pretty impressive. They could both be winners.

He pulled on his pajamas, then glanced in the mirror and frowned at his reflection. He knew everyone thought he was a hero, but all he saw was a zero.

He wasn't really a hero, and he knew it deep down.

I'm a fraud, he thought.

Suddenly, the blue flame flashed in the mirror.

A deep, smarmy voice echoed through the room.

"Liar, Liar, Head on Fire!"

Hades erupted into bright red flames in the mirror. The mirror shattered from the blast of heat, glass shards flying everywhere.

Hector leapt back, protecting his eyes from the glass. Inky, black smoke poured out of the shattered mirror, filling his bedroom and choking him.

Hector coughed, unable to breathe. His eyes stung from it. His throat felt like it was burning. Red and orange flames licked out of the mirror, kissing his face.

Hector burst out of his bedroom and bolted to the kitchen, expecting the smoke alarm to blare and gasping for breath.

The smoke chased him down the hall, following him like a ghost.

He could feel the heat behind him starting to devour the house. Soon it would go up in flames. His family was in danger.

"Help! Call nine-one-one!" he screamed to his family. "We have to get out! My room is on fire!"

13
LIAR, LIAR, HEAD ON FIRE

"**H**urry, call for help!"

Hector burst into the kitchen, shouting. His heart hammered in his chest. His lungs burned from the thick smoke.

His family turned to look at him in surprise. His parents were at the sink, working in tandem, Mom washing the dishes and Dad drying them. Juan and Luca played on their phones at the table while Phil finished clearing the plates.

"Uh, honey," Mom said, pulling her soapy hands out of the sink and looking worried. "What're you talking about?"

"The fire . . . don't you see it?" Hector said. "The smoke?"

He trailed off and glanced back toward his room. The door gaped open.

But there was nothing.

No smoke. No fire. No voice.

He inhaled, smelling the air, but it was clear and unpolluted.

His family all shot him strange looks. Juan made a cuckoo sign with his fingers to Luca, making him crack up. Mom shot them a look that said—*Hey, cut it out.*

Dad wiped his hands on a towel and came over, pressing his warm hands to Hector's forehead.

"Son, you feeling okay?" he asked. "You've been acting kind of strange since you won the race."

"Yeah, like, stranger than normal," Phil chimed in, setting down the dirty dishes he was clearing near the sink. "And that's saying a lot."

"Wh-what do you mean?" Hector said, his heart still thumping with adrenaline.

Phil scratched his head. He spent more time with

Hector than the rest of the family. "Let's see, like jumpy and agitated, but also arrogant and full of yourself. Total mood swings."

Dad chuckled. "Sounds like typical teen stuff. Is that it?"

"I mean, he's, like, twelve going on sixteen," Mom added with a knowing shake of her head.

"Yeah, and he's been talking to a girl," Luca added, ratting him out. "I caught him texting her."

"Me, too," Juan added. "I saw his phone. Her name is Mae."

Hector swallowed hard. He knew his moodiness was far more than typical. And it had nothing to do with texting Mae or normal teen stuff. He and Mae were just friends anyway.

No. What he was dealing with was not normal. He was seeing smoke and fires that weren't there. Not to mention talking to demons. Hearing voices. There was only one explanation.

Hades was haunting him. Because Hector broke their deal.

Suddenly, upsetting the God of the Underworld

didn't seem like such a great idea. He should've given him the Zeus Cup.

But he couldn't tell his family any of this. They were so proud of him. He couldn't stand to disappoint them. Plus, it was unlikely they'd believe him. They'd just think he was going crazy.

"Uh, you're right," Hector said, forcing the lie out. "I'm probably just tired and stressed. There's been a lot of pressure on me."

Dad rubbed his shoulders. "Son, you just need to get a good night of sleep. I promise you'll feel better tomorrow."

He turned to Phil. "Will you help your brother get to bed?"

Phil led Hector back to his bedroom. "Hey, I know you're going through a lot. But I want you to know you can talk to me. I'm here for you . . . always."

Hector's heart flooded with guilt. He hadn't exactly been that nice to his brother today. They reached his room, and Phil helped him settle into bed. Hector slid under the worn sheets, still feeling totally unsettled. He felt . . . haunted.

"Look, I'm sorry I've been acting all weird today,"

Hector started. "I thought winning the Zeus Cup would make everything better. But it's all so confusing."

"Well, it's just a trophy," Phil said. "I thought it mattered a lot, too. But what matters is that you worked so hard and earned it."

That made Hector feel even worse. If his brother knew he had cheated to win . . .

"But I didn't work that hard," Hector sputtered, feeling his mood shift. "Listen, you don't understand. I don't deserve it."

Hector's words hung in the air. Phil gave him a look.

"You know, I never thought I'd say this," Phil confessed, shaking his head. "Because I know I pushed you super hard to win the Cup. But I liked you better before."

Hector felt like he'd been punched in the stomach.

"You mean, when I was a zero?" he snapped. "And nobody cared about me? You're just jealous because I won—and you never did."

Phil flinched, then just shook his head sadly. "Hector, you were never a zero."

"Easy for you to say," Hector shot back. "How would you know?"

Phil gave him a squeeze on the shoulder and met his eyes.

"Because you've always been my brother," he said in a soft voice. "A true hero isn't measured by the size of his strength—but the strength of his heart."

14
PLAYING HOOKY

"**N**o, leave me alone!" Hector screamed, bolting up, gasping for air, and clawing at his throat.

That night, his dreams had been filled with fire and smoke and devilish voices. His last nightmare ended with a strange image—the moon, sun, and all the planets coming into perfect alignment, like a super eclipse.

He woke up sweaty and more tired than when he went to sleep. He squinted at the morning light flooding his little room. His lungs burned from breathing smoke, even though it had just been a dream.

Except, maybe it hadn't.

Hector knew better now. Hades was real—and clearly,

he wasn't happy that Hector had backed out of their deal.

But the Zeus Cup was locked up at Hero's. And his mom had the key.

There was no way he could take it back now. Business was booming at Hero's ever since he had won the Cup. People came in just to take pictures of themselves with the trophy case, and inevitably, they'd end up browsing and buying something.

The image from his dream of the planets lingered in his mind. What did it all mean?

He slid out of bed and studied his reflection in the mirror. He was still possessed with superstrength, but his face looked haggard. Dark circles lined his eyes. His skin appeared sallow.

He looked haunted.

His body was strong, but he felt like he was losing his mind, and he didn't know what to do about it. His family didn't seem to understand. And he didn't have any friends . . . except for one.

Mae.

Hector felt sick at the idea of telling her what he'd done to beat her. He mulled it over, watching his face in the mirror. He couldn't go on like this much longer. He had to do something.

He had to tell someone.

And she was his only friend. What choice did he have?

* * *

Hector searched all over town for Mae, finally finding her at the place he should've looked first.

The track.

She was sweaty and running laps, training with hurdles. She leapt over them with a natural grace and ease that Hector envied. He dug out his camera from its bag and snapped some candid pictures of her running.

When Mae crossed the finish line, she doubled over to catch her breath. Hector stowed his camera quickly.

"Mae! Hi!" Hector waved to get her attention.

Mae looked up and her eyes narrowed. She didn't look happy to see him, that was for sure.

"Hey there," she said as Hector loped toward her. "What're you doing here? I thought you were busy with your fans these days."

"Oh, please," Hector said. "I thought it would be so

cool to win, but I can't go one square block without getting stopped and asked for a selfie or an autograph."

Mae scowled. "Yeah, sounds totally awful. I don't know how you cope."

Hector's stomach sank. This wasn't going well. He kept putting his foot in his mouth.

"Still training? Not even taking a little time off?" he tried again, following her as she walked the track to cool down. His camera bag thumped heavily against his hip.

"Track tryouts are in two weeks," she replied, stretching her arms overhead as she walked. "No playing hooky. Not for me."

"You never take a break?" he asked, frowning.

Mae shook her head. Her tough facade seemed to soften a bit.

"I lost the race, so Dad's been pushing me extra hard to train for this upcoming track season. All my parents care about is *winning*."

Hector paused. "And what do you care about?"

She turned to look at him, and bit her lower lip. "Follow me," she said finally. "I'll show you."

* * *

Mae led him to her house on the outskirts of town. They jogged together, so it didn't take long to get there.

Mae lived in a ranch house like Hector's, but it had a sprawling, tree-lined backyard filled with a track and training equipment—rope climbs, hurdles, benches and weights, even a brick wall and mud trap.

Mae caught him checking out the backyard practice field.

"Home sweet home," she said, then smirked. "Or more like, home sweet track."

"Wow, I'll say," Hector remarked, admiring the training equipment. Some of it clearly came from Hero's, but a lot of it was custom-built. He ran his hands over a wooden balance beam, admiring it. "Who made all this stuff?"

"My dad did," Mae said. "He really does love me. He just doesn't understand me, I guess."

Hector nodded. "I know what that feels like. Are they home?"

"They're both at work," Mae said, leading him inside. "Mom will be home soon, but Dad works the night shift so he has time to train me during the day. Today he had to do a double cuz he took some time off for the big race."

Inside, the differences between Mae's house and his own were even more apparent. For starters, Mae was an only child, so it looked less well-trodden. The furniture was fancier and less worn, too.

"This is where the magic happens," Mae said, leading him into the finished basement. "Or rather, the music."

She flicked a switch and light flooded the space, illuminating stands with shiny electric guitars in a range of colors, as well as amps, mixing boards, and other equipment. The floors were concrete covered with carpeting. The walls had foam tiling to soundproof the room.

All around the basement were posters of famous rock bands — old-school stuff like Nirvana and Green Day, but also newer punk bands that Hector didn't recognize. They looked fierce. His parents and Phil loved '90s music, too.

"I should've been born in the '90s," Mae said with a whimsical shake of her head. She fondled the neck of a cherry-red guitar. It gleamed under the lights. "Kurt used to play this kind. He's a legend."

"If your parents don't want you playing music, then why do you have all this stuff?" Hector asked.

"I use my Christmases and birthdays wisely," Mae said

with a shrewd smile. "My mom made my dad put in the soundproofing."

"Not bad." Hector grinned. "That's a cool guitar. I'd love to hear you play."

"I dunno," Mae said, blushing. "I'm kind of shy."

Shy? Was she kidding? She'd never acted that way on the track. But then, Hector understood. He felt shy about his photography, too. It was because this was what she actually loved. Music was her true passion.

"Well, how do you expect to join a band if you can't even play for me?" he teased. "I'm your friend. It's my job to be nice and cheer for you, no matter what."

She took a deep breath and flicked on the amp. It buzzed fiercely with feedback, then chilled out. Slowly, she strapped on the red guitar.

When she started to play, raucous electric guitar chords filled the basement room with their rich sound. Her fingers flew over the neck of the guitar, expertly coaxing out notes from the strings.

Hector couldn't believe his ears. He knew that Mae loved to play music, but witnessing her devotion to it was a whole other level. Without thinking, he pulled out his camera.

He started snapping photographs like a rock-music photographer. She gave him a questioning look, but then she got into it, even posing for him.

She finished the song, breaking into a rad looping guitar solo at the end, then flashing devil horns.

"Wow, you're amazing," Hector said, clapping for her. "You're a total rock star!"

Mae blushed, flicking off the amp's power. "You just said that you're required to cheer no matter what. How can I believe you?"

"Okay, fair enough," Hector said with a laugh. "But seriously, you're so talented. You should join a band! I'd totally go see you."

Her face fell. "I would love to, but I can't with my training schedule. My dad won't allow it. He says I can't afford to get distracted."

She unstrapped the guitar and set it down, then met his eyes.

A moment passed between them—a solidifying of

their friendship. Hector could feel it. It gave him the courage to tell her the reason he'd tracked her down.

"Mae, there's something I need to tell you . . ." He trailed off.

"I figured," she said with a snort. "You've been acting all weird and nervous. I guessed something was up."

"Yeah, but it's not going to be easy," he said, looking away and fiddling with the knobs on his camera. "Maybe it's a bad idea."

"No, you can tell me anything. Heck, I just whaled on guitar for you. You know my secret."

"Yeah, but this is different," he hedged, his stomach twisting.

She crossed her arms. "Now you *have* to tell me. You're freaking me out."

"You promise to still be my friend?" Hector said. "No matter what?"

"Of course," she said without hesitation. "Best friends forever."

Hector took a deep breath, then confessed everything. His fear about losing the Zeus Cup to her after his defeat in the preliminary race, the demons showing up in his bedroom, making the deal with Hades but then backing out.

The more he talked, the wider her eyes got. When he finished, he flexed his arms to show her his muscle tone. The gifts that Hades bestowed on him still worked.

"Wait, that's how you won the race—you cheated?" Mae said, her face twisting with anger that shifted to vindication. "Wow, I knew you did something! I just couldn't figure out what."

"You did?" Hector said, feeling even worse. "How'd you know?"

"Well, you got so much faster and stronger basically overnight," she said. "It just didn't make sense. That flip you did at the wall? There was no way that was something you normally did."

She paced around, agitated. "Ugh! I'd never have guessed it was a deal with a Greek god, though. I mean, that's crazy! I was thinking maybe you had too much caffeine that morning or something, not that you had magic."

"Yeah, well, now you know the truth," Hector said. "But listen, it was a mistake. It's awful. Now Hades won't leave me alone. The trophy is locked up in my family's store. I can't get it out to give it to him. What am I going to do?"

He sank down to his knees, feeling the full weight of every single mistake that he'd made. But the last thought hurt the most.

"Also, now you're not going to be my friend anymore," he said. "And I can't blame you. What I did was wrong. That trophy should belong to you."

He felt tears prick his eyes and swallowed hard against them, making his throat feel thick. Mae was his only friend in the world, and now he'd lost her.

Mae glared at him. "You're right—the Cup should be mine." But then her face softened. "But also, I get it—and I forgive you."

"Wait, what do you mean?" Hector said, looking up in surprise. "You're not mad? You're still my friend?"

"Oh, I'm super raging at you right now. But in your position, I'd have done the same thing," she confessed. "I'd have done anything to win, just like you."

"Still friends?" Hector said with a hard swallow.

"Yup, still friends," she agreed. "Even though I'm gonna be annoyed at you for a bit. And I might have to find a way to get back at you," she finished with a good-hearted chuckle.

"Deal," Hector said right away.

He felt like the heavy weight that had been draped across his shoulders had lifted. He couldn't believe it. Lying felt like dragging extra pounds around all the time. But the truth felt light as a feather. He shot Mae a grateful look, but then his face fell again.

"Thanks, but I'm in so much trouble," he went on. "I didn't give the Zeus Cup to Hades—and now the God of the Underworld is after me."

Mae thought it over, then frowned. "Why does Hades want the trophy so bad?"

Hector searched back in his memory to that night. "He said something about some old feud with his brother. He said it was just a bunch of god stuff."

"God stuff, huh?" Mae said, pondering it. "The Zeus Cup must have important powers, or he wouldn't want it so bad. Right?"

"Yeah, that's true," Hector agreed.

"Think back to that night," Mae prodded. "What did Hades say about the Zeus Cup?"

Hector furrowed his brow. "Let's see, Hades said something about it being . . . the key to getting out of the Underworld."

Mae looked up sharply. "The key?"

Hector nodded. "Yes, I think he used that exact word. What do you think it means?"

"Well, I don't know what it means," Mae said. "But I do know one thing. We need to find out more about the Zeus Cup—and there's only one place to look."

Hector scratched his head uncertainly. "Where's that?"

Mae grabbed her bag. "Where this all started."

15
LORD OF THE DEAD

"**S**o this is where you wanted to take me?" Hector asked, peering up at the imposing white marble statue of Hades, which stared back at them impassively. The very sight of it gave him chills.

They stood in the town square's little park, shrouded by leafy trees and surrounded by the statues of the Greek gods. In a certain light, the statues appeared so lifelike that it almost felt like the gods were watching them—and not very happily. Hector glanced over at Zeus. The god looked regal on his throne and clutched a lightning bolt in his hand.

My brothers can be super annoying, Hector thought. *But I'd never imprison any of them in the Underworld.*

He wondered what Hades had done to make Zeus so angry. From what he knew, the Greek gods always seemed to have a lot of family drama going on, not unlike the reality TV shows that his mother loved. Dad pretended to find his mom's shows annoying, but he was always glued to the screen when he thought nobody was looking.

"Well, isn't this where you said it started?" Mae said, gazing up at the Hades statue. "The demons brought you here. You said the statue came to life, right?" she added, circling it slowly and studying it. "And Hades started talking to you?"

She ran her hands over the smooth marble surface, searching for clues. Hades' frozen face peered down at them, unmoving. Hector felt a jolt of fear, remembering how the statue's yellow eyes had popped open and his head ignited with bright, blue flames.

Hector half expected the statue to come to life again, just like it did that fateful night. But the statue remained still.

"Yeah . . ." he said nervously. "And well, he's kind of scary. Not sure it's a good idea to bother him—"

"Hey, knock-knock!" Mae called out, ignoring Hector's

warning and rapping on the statue. "Anybody home? Yo, Lord of the Dead? Wake up! We wanna talk to you!"

"Uh, I think he prefers *God of the Underworld*," Hector quipped.

"Scary god dude . . . whatever," Mae said, rolling her eyes. She knocked on the marble again. "You in there?"

Hector braced himself for Hades to awaken, but nothing happened.

The statue didn't move.

The eyes didn't light up.

The hair didn't ignite.

While Mae inspected it further, Hector snapped pictures of Hades, as well as the other statues in the park. He caught his lens drifting to Mae, capturing some candid pics of her.

"Well, it just seems like a normal statue to me," Mae said finally, stumped. She bit her lower lip. "Or he doesn't want to talk to us."

Hector lowered his camera, feeling both disappointed and relieved. They retreated to a park bench, where they shared some snacks that Hector kept stowed in his camera bag.

"Got any other ideas?" he asked. He wasn't sure what he was hoping they'd find, but he hoped it'd be something that would help.

"Lemme see the pictures you took," Mae said, popping a peanut-butter cracker into her mouth. "Maybe there's a clue if we look closer."

Hector pulled up the images that he'd snapped of Hades on the digital screen. They flicked through them, inspecting the different angles.

Hades' frozen face flashed across the digital screen, then suddenly—

The camera starting acting up. It started to turn *warm*.

"Uh, do you feel that?" Hector said, pulling Mae's hand to touch it.

"Ouch!" she said, yelping and yanking it back. "Maybe the battery's overheating. Try turning it off."

But then something about the image of Hades changed. Its eyes lit up with searing yellow light.

"What's happening?" Mae said, jumping back in fear.

But Hector couldn't look away. The camera stayed locked in his grip, as if glued to his hands . . . or more like melted into them.

It grew hotter, burning his palms. "Ouch, it's burning me!"

"Put the camera down!" Mae said. "Hurry up! Drop it!"

"I'm trying, but I can't let go!" Hector managed, wincing in pain. "My hands are stuck to it!"

Suddenly, the Hades statue came to life in the picture, gnashing his pointy teeth and snarling at them. His voice boomed out.

"The Zeus Cup belongs to me!"

Smoke started drifting out of the camera's lens, stinging their eyes and making them cough.

Then suddenly—

Red flames surged out of the camera's screen at their faces.

"Hurry, turn it off!" Mae yelled.

"I can't!"

The flames seared his face, making his cheeks burn, while the camera singed his hands. Mae finally lunged toward him and hit the POWER button, then pulled her hand back to shake it out as if burned.

The flames and smoke vanished, retracting into

the camera almost as if sucked into a flue, as the screen went dark.

Hector dropped the camera onto the bench and stared at the black screen. His heart thumped and his breath came in staccato bursts, like when he snapped rapid-fire pictures. His hands still tingled and felt hot from the camera burning them, but they were quickly returning to normal.

"What was that?" Hector said, struggling to catch his breath.

"I have no idea!" Mae said. "But wow, you weren't kidding! That Hades dude isn't very friendly."

"Wait, you could see all that?" Hector said, the last few intense moments finally coming into focus for him. "The smoke? The fire? Hades coming to life?"

"Uh, yeah?" Mae said. "You're right, he's kind of scary. Actually, *kind of scary* doesn't do him justice. I'd say more like, mega scary. Terrifying. Petrifying."

"And you could hear him, too?" Hector said, excited.

"Yeah, he wants the Zeus Cup pretty bad," Mae said with wide eyes. "He sounded angry, too."

"Wow, I feel so much better," Hector said, exhaling in relief.

"Better?" Mae said. "How could you possibly feel better? You've managed to enrage the Lord of the Dead. I'd say that's a pretty bad situation."

"I know, but you can see and hear it, too!" Hector said excitedly. "At least I'm not losing it. Nobody else can see him. At least, not my family."

"Well, I wouldn't blame you for losing it," Mae said. "An ancient, mega-scary Greek god dude is haunting you. I'd be going a little nuts, too, if I were you."

Hector touched the camera. It still felt warm, but it had cooled off a bit. It looked completely normal, though. Which made no sense at all. It had basically burst into flames two minutes ago, yet it was completely intact.

"What do you think it means?" he asked, glancing at Mae.

She chewed her lower lip thoughtfully.

"Somebody doesn't want us snooping around his statue," she said, sounding concerned. Her gaze flicked over to Hades. "What do you think he doesn't want us to know?"

16
RELEASE
THE TITANS

Hector breathed in—and smelled them. Books, books, and more books. His eyes scanned the cozy wood-paneled, shelf-lined space lit by overhead fluorescent lights.

"Don't you just love that smell?" Mae said, leading him deeper inside the library.

Hector started to agree, but then he sneezed.

"Yeah, except when they trigger my allergies," he said.

They both laughed, but then Mae's expression turned serious. They were here for a reason, and just thinking about it made Hector feel anxious.

"This way," Mae said, pulling his arm and leading him

all the way to the back of the library. His eyes scanned the shelves as they passed, taking in the musty books.

"Where're we going?" he asked. "I think the history section is that way. Or maybe we need mythology?"

She shook her head. "No, there's a special section. We should start there."

"Special section?" Hector repeated. Truthfully, he'd never spent that much time in the library. His spare time was spent on the training field.

"Yup, should be right over here," Mae said, halting in front of a wooden door. The sign at its center read:

CURATED BY THE
MT. OLYMPUS HISTORICAL SOCIETY

"There's a special section dedicated to our town's history and the Mt. Olympus Spartan Run," Mae told Hector, twisting the handle and leading him inside.

The room was filled with books, maps, and historical documents. Comfortable chairs and sofas were placed around the room. There were three ancient computers on desks set against the back wall.

"Wow, how did you know about this?" Hector asked, scanning the space. He approached a map encased in glass, studying the town layout.

"Dad made me do a research paper on the Spartan race," she said with an exaggerated eye roll. "He wanted me to understand how important it was and learn the history. He said training is as much mental as it is physical."

"Hard-core," Hector said. "And also, super true. I grew up in a family totally obsessed with it, so I started learning about the Zeus Cup before I could even crawl."

Hector explored the room. Displayed on one wall were black-and-white photographs depicting the construction of the town center. His eyes fixed on the pictures showing the marble statues being hoisted by a crane and installed in the park. He loved how photos could preserve a moment in time—or in this case—in history.

"Check this out," Mae said, calling him over to one of the tables. She had a large book open in front of her. "According to this, the original founders of our town emigrated here from Greece."

"Everyone knows that," Hector said. "They brought the marble statues, too."

"Yup, exactly." Mae nodded, flipping through the book. "But that's not all they brought over."

The next page showed an old photograph of the Zeus Cup. Mae's eyes lit up excitedly.

"They brought the Zeus Cup?" Hector said. "Wow, then it could be really old. Ancient, even."

"Exactly," Mae said, scanning the pages. "But there's more. It says here that the founders of the town brought the Zeus Cup over here from Greece . . . to hide it."

"But why would they need to hide it?" Hector said.

"Hades," Mae said, her face turning darker. She flipped to the next page. Hector started back in fear—it was a painting of Zeus and Hades battling as Zeus tried to imprison his brother in the Underworld. But that wasn't what caught Hector's eye.

Two little demons clung to Hades' legs as Zeus was about to strike him with a lightning bolt.

They were the same demons that had visited him in his bedroom that night and led him to the Hades statue.

Pain and Panic.

"That's them!" Hector said, pointing to the demons.

"They're the ones that brought me to Hades in the first place!"

"They're his minions," Mae said, reading the description. "It says they serve Hades."

"I can't believe this is happening," Hector said. "It's impossible."

"I can't believe your camera tried to burn you alive," Mae said, giving him a pointed look. "I think we left impossible behind a long time ago."

"Good point." Hector followed her gaze to the next section. It was all about the town's Spartan Run.

"Look here," Mae said. "According to this, the Mt. Olympus Spartan Run originated in ancient Greece. It was a test to select the best protector for the Zeus Cup."

"A test?" Hector said, thinking it over.

Mae continued reading. "The victor in the race was supposed to be the strongest and bravest—the hero most suited to keep the Zeus Cup safe. . . ."

"And out of Hades' greedy hands," Hector finished.

"Yup, it makes sense," Mae said. "They wanted to find a way to protect it. Why not a race?"

Hector's stomach filled with dread. "And I've completely failed as a hero."

"No, Hades tempted you into making a deal," Mae said emphatically, meeting his eyes. "That's what he does—he manipulates mortals. He's also a liar. You can't trust him."

Mae pulled down another book—this one titled *The God of the Underworld*. The cover even looked scary, with flames and demons surrounding Hades.

"Hate to tell you this," Mae said, flipping through the book on the Lord of the Dead, "but he's a pretty bad dude."

"Ugh. Tell me something I don't know," Hector said, scanning the pages.

Images of the Underworld flashed before his eyes, making him shudder in fear. The Land of the Dead resembled a cavernous, underground hellscape constantly burning with fires and populated with ghastly monsters. They were the creatures of nightmares.

Their fearsome visages flashed before his eyes as Mae flipped the pages. One looked like a ferocious three-headed dog. Its name was *Cerberus*. Apparently, Cerberus was the guard of the Underworld and served Hades. Another creature had a number of heads as well, but it looked like a water serpent. Its name was *Hydra*.

This creature lived in a river that flowed through the Underworld named the River Styx, where Hades imprisoned the souls of mortals for all eternity, after their lifeline was cut by the Fates.

Mae flipped to the next page and scanned it. "Look here, according to this book, releasing the Titans is Hades' main obsession," she said, pointing to images of the creatures.

The Titans looked like monsters. There was really no other word for them.

And they had incredible powers. According to the book, the Titans were gods who ruled before Zeus, also known as pre-Olympian gods, who had been imprisoned for many millennia. They would serve whoever released them, and once freed, they would dethrone Zeus, take over Mt. Olympus, and destroy the world.

The Mountain King: a two-headed Titan made completely out of rock.

The Lurker: an ice monster.

The Lord of Flame: a lava creature.

The Mystic Voice: a being made of wind, like a tornado.

And the worst one—*Cyclops*. This was an enormous, bloblike pink one-eyed monster.

"Wait, so it's not just god stuff?" Hector said, his eyes fixed on the giants' monstrous faces. Cyclops stared back with his single eyeball. The illustration was so lifelike that Hector had to look away. "Hades wants to release the Titans when he escapes from the Underworld?"

Mae nodded. "Yeah, Hades lied to you. It's not just god stuff. If he escapes from the Underworld in time for the Celestial Alignment that's coming up tonight..." She tapped an image of the planets all aligned in a cosmic row. "He can release the Titans."

"And they'll destroy the world," Hector finished.

His words echoed in the room, then silence enfolded them. Hector could tell they were both thinking the same thing.

We can't let Hades get the Zeus Cup—we have to protect it.

"But what am I going to do?" Hector said, standing up and pacing around the room. Fear rippled through him.

"You saw what happened with my camera. It's getting worse, especially with the alignment coming up. Hades isn't going to leave me alone."

Mae bit her lip. "I don't know. I'll check out this book. Maybe it'll have a clue as to his weaknesses. Something we can use against him. There must be some way to defeat him and make it stop—"

"Smell that?" Hector said, feeling his nose prickle— and it wasn't allergies this time.

"Smoke." Mae gulped.

"It's Hades—he's here!" Hector gasped, wheeling around. Smoke wafted into the library, gushing out of the shelves. It choked them and blocked the light.

Suddenly, flames erupted from the books and engulfed the bookshelf behind him. A shadowy, demonic figure rose up out of the framed picture of Hades on the wall.

"Fools! Mortals!" Hades' shadowy figure shouted. "You can't stop me! I'm a god—I'm immortal! Only another god can defeat me!"

17
JEEPERS, MISTER!

Hades' shadowy figure burst out of the painting and rose up over them, blue flames sprouting from his head. As he loomed forward, the flames erupted, turning orange, then red.

That meant he was angry.

Like, really, really angry.

Hades' shadow thrust out his arms, knocking against the flaming bookshelf. The enormous shelf wobbled, then crashed toward Hector and Mae, threatening to crush them. Flaming books tumbled out and hit the floor at their feet.

"Watch out!" Hector said, grabbing Mae's arm and yanking her out of the way. "Run!"

They both had great reflexes and dodged the flaming bookshelf just as it collapsed. Ash, sparks, and embers exploded into the air.

"Hurry! Run!" Hector cried, pulling Mae toward the door. The smoke made his eyes water and his lungs burn and scream for oxygen. Stars danced in his vision.

Beep! Beep! Beep!

The fire alarm sounded its shrill cry, but no one was coming to help.

Hector risked a glance back. Behind them, the books burned on their shelves, catching fire like dry tinder and spreading. The whole room was quickly going up in flames.

But that wasn't the worst part.

"The Zeus Cup belongs to me!"

Hades' demonic shadow chased after them.

His shadowy hands reached out their clawed fingers—

Hector yanked the door open just in time. He and Mae burst through it, slamming it shut behind them with a loud *bang*.

Patrons in the main library looked up from their

reading and browsing with puzzled expressions. "Shhhhhh!" the librarian hissed at them.

Hector's mouth dropped open. He was about to say— *Call the fire department!* But then he shut his mouth. They couldn't see it. They couldn't hear it or smell it or anything.

He turned back toward the blazing inferno they'd left in the specialized history section of the library. Mae followed his gaze.

There was no smoke seeping out from under the door. No fire alarm blaring. No demonic shadow chasing after them.

Hector felt his cheeks flame, this time from embarrassment. Mae looked freaked out, too. She glanced around the library at the patrons staring back at them in irritation.

"Why can't they see it?" she stammered in a low voice. "But we can?"

"I don't know," Hector said. "But let's get out of here."

* * *

They burst outside into the bright sunlight. The sun would start to set soon, casting the sky into twilight and a burst of sunset colors, much like embers. The sky would look like it was on fire.

Mae still looked scared. She was breathing heavily. "Okay, Hades is way freakier than you mentioned. No wonder Zeus trapped him in the Underworld."

Hector nodded. "Yeah, well, that was way worse than normal. And normal was already pretty terrifying. He's getting angrier."

"Yeah, because he's running out of time," Mae said. "That Celestial Alignment is coming up tonight, according to the book. I was gonna read more about it—"

"Ugh, we left the book behind," Hector said in despair. He wheeled back toward the library, but he was pretty sure going back there was a bad idea.

On top of everything else, the librarian seemed pretty annoyed by their screaming and stampeding through the stacks. If Hades didn't kill him for coming back, she probably would.

Hades was scary—but librarians could be scarier

if you disturbed their precious peace and quiet, not to mention their books.

Mae shot him a look, then arched her eyebrow.

"No, we didn't," she said.

"Wait, what do you mean?" Hector asked.

She produced the *Lord of the Underworld* book from under her shirt. She'd smuggled it out.

Hector shot her an impressed look. "Playing dirty to win, huh?"

"Sometimes you have to," Mae said with a smirk. "Too much is at stake. Maybe even the whole world."

Hector was forced to agree—the fate of the world rested in their hands. They had to defeat Hades and keep him from getting the Zeus Cup, or he'd release the Titans and destroy the earth.

They started back toward Hector's house as the sun was sinking. Hector didn't like what night would bring. He glanced at the stars, picturing the planets aligning in a cosmic row, providing Hades the ability to release the Titans if he got out.

As they passed through downtown and under the awning

for Hero's, Hector peered inside at the Zeus Cup, illuminated in the case. Clearly Hades couldn't take it for himself, or have Pain and Panic do it for him, or he would have grabbed it by now. Only Hector, it seemed, could deliver it to the god, and his mom kept the key with her at all times, so it was secure.

For now.

"Who knew one little trophy could cause so much trouble?" Mae said thoughtfully, following his gaze.

"Yeah, and *pain* and *panic*," Hector quipped.

They both laughed. Maybe he was turning into his dad with his sense of humor, after all.

"But it did do something good," Mae added wistfully.

Hector met her eyes. "Oh yeah? What's that?"

"It brought us together," Mae said, reaching out to squeeze his hand. "I never told you this. But before you, I never had a real friend."

"Wait, what do you mean?" Hector said. "You go to the public school. You must have a ton of them."

Mae shook her head. "Hard to hang out when you're always at the track. The other kids don't understand." She bit her lip. "But you do."

"Yeah, more than I'd like to admit," he agreed. "Well,

if we're confessing. Before you, I never really had a friend, either."

"Really?" she said, sounding surprised.

"Unless you count my brothers. But they have to like me," he added with a self-deprecating laugh. "You're different."

They rounded the corner and heard yelling. It sounded like two kids, and they sounded like they were in trouble. It was coming from off the side of the road.

"Help! We're stuck!" yelled one kid. "Hurry, call nine-one-one!"

"Please, save us!" yelled the other one. "We're trapped!"

Mae grabbed his arm. "Do you hear that?"

They bolted off the road, toward the woods. The kids' shrill voices were coming from under a giant boulder. It looked like they'd climbed into a hole and got stuck.

"We have to help them," Mae said. "But how?"

Hector felt a surge of strength travel through his body. He still had the powers that Hades had bestowed upon him.

"Here's the plan," he said. "I'm going to lift the boulder, then you get the kids out, okay?"

"You can lift that?" Mae said. "It's huge. It must weigh, like, a million pounds."

Hector bent down, braced his legs, and pushed his hands under the boulder, gripping it. Then he grunted and dead-lifted the giant rock, pushing it up and off of the trapped kids.

Mae looked shocked, but then quickly sprang into action.

"Here, give me your hand!" she called, helping the first kid wriggle out. He was blond and chubby with rosy cheeks.

Mae helped the other kid, who was taller and skinny with dark skin and hair.

"Careful, I've got you!" she said, pulling him to safety as well.

"Everyone good?" Hector asked.

Mae nodded, and Hector released the boulder, letting it crash down.

"How'd you do that?" Mae said, wide-eyed.

"Hades gave me powers, remember?" Hector said. "At least I was able to use them for good."

"Like a true hero," Mae said.

They turned to the kids, who held on to each other, trembling.

"Jeepers, mister!" the shorter one said. "You saved us!"

"How can we thank you?" the skinny kid added.

Hector felt good, like he'd just done something right for once. Plus, he made a great team with Mae. He grinned at her, but then the two kids pounced on Mae.

"No, get off me!" she yelled, fighting them. But the kids were stronger—*too strong*.

"Hey, what're you doing?" Hector yelled. "We saved you!"

"Stirring performance, don't you think?" the skinny one said.

"Yeah, I was going for innocence," the chubby one added.

They clapped their hands over Mae's face to stifle her screams, and started dragging her away.

"Wh-what do you mean?" Hector stammered.

Suddenly, like magic, the kids morphed into Pain and Panic. Hector couldn't believe what he was seeing.

The two demons stared back at him with their yellow

eyes. "Bring Hades the Zeus Cup before the Celestial Alignment at midnight," Panic said.

"Yeah, or you can kiss your little friend here good-bye," Pain added, wriggling his claws.

The demons dragged Mae away into the forest. Hector chased after them, branches smacking his face, and cornered them in a small clearing.

"Let her go!" Hector said, preparing to fight them off. "Where are you taking her?"

Mae squirmed in their clawed grip, trying to get free. Panic leveled his gaze on Hector.

"It's the girl for the Cup," he said.

"You have until midnight," Pain added in his goofy voice. "Or the Boss Man keeps her soul trapped in the River Styx—"

"Shut up!" Panic said, shooting Pain a look. "You weren't supposed to tell him that!"

"Oh right!" Pain said. "Hurry, let's skedaddle before he figures it out!"

With that, Panic threw down a potion. The bottle exploded, and the demons vanished in a puff of pink smoke, taking Mae with them.

18
WORK OF HEART

"**N**o! Please!" Hector shouted.

He coughed from the smoke, waving it away, trying to grab Pain or Panic or Mae or *anything*.

But they were gone.

Hades' demons had kidnapped Mae. Pain and Panic were aptly named. They did cause pain and panic wherever they went.

This was all Hector's fault. If he hadn't made the deal with Hades, then Mae would be okay. He didn't know what to do. He stood in the clearing, feeling hopeless. This was worse than when he lost the preliminary race to Mae. Worse than when Hades started haunting his every step.

It was worse because it wasn't just about him anymore—it was about his best friend.

His only friend.

Mae, I'm going to save you.

But how? he wondered, surveying the woods. The sun was starting to descend in the sky. That meant he didn't have much time left. Also, he didn't know where the demons had taken her. Where could he even start?

He thought back to what Pain and Panic had said, racking his brain, and then it hit him. They said they'd trap her soul in the River Styx. He remembered seeing illustrations of the fiery river in the book Mae had stolen from the library. He knew where the river was located.

In the Underworld.

That's where they were taking her. That's where Hades was holding her hostage.

All he had to do was get the Zeus Cup by breaking it out of his family's store, and then somehow find the door to the Underworld, so that he could give it to Hades and rescue Mae.

But Hector hesitated—releasing Hades from the Underworld could be bad. Like, world-ending, cataclysmic kind of bad. He shuddered, remembering the images of the Titans from the book in the library.

But he had to save Mae.

Maybe there was a way to save her and still keep the Zeus Cup out of Hades' hands. Hades manipulated mortals—he tricked them. Maybe Hector could do the same thing.

He'd have to play dirty to win this time.

And he only had a few hours to do it.

* * *

Hector had a plan, but he needed help. And there was only one person left that he trusted.

He found Phil lounging on his bed, playing video games. He was the oldest—and the only brother who had a TV and PlayStation in his room.

"Phil, I need your help," Hector said, rapping on the door.

"This is my week off," Phil said. "Stop bothering me, Wonderboy. All I want to do is veg out and play my Hercules RPG. Don't you have autographs to go sign?"

He swiped at demons in the game with a flaming sword.

"Look, I'm sorry for how I've been acting," Hector said, feeling remorse pooling in his chest. "I know I let winning the Cup go to my head. And I'm sorry. It was a mistake."

"You got that right," Phil said, not looking up. "And I'm never going to forgive you."

"What . . . never?" Hector said in surprise. He often fought with his brothers, but one rule in the Gomez family was that you always forgave each other after.

But then Phil cracked a smile. "Nah, I'm just messing with you!" he said, grabbing Hector and giving him a solid noogie for good measure. Hector's scalp burned, but he deserved it.

"Hey, freak, get off me!" Hector giggled, swiping at Phil. He rubbed his head.

They both laughed hard, then settled down. "So, what do you need?" Phil said, cocking his eyebrow. "Figure it must be important for you to come in here and grovel like this."

"Uh, well, I need to get the Zeus Cup out of the trophy case," Hector started. He felt a stab of nervousness, but plowed ahead. "And Mom and Dad can't know about it."

Phil frowned. "Why do you need the Cup?"

"Uh, I can't tell you," Hector said. "You won't believe me."

Phil broke into a sly smile. "Oh, I get it. Juan and Luca were right. You wanna impress some girl, is that it?"

"No, that's not it," Hector started, his cheeks burning with humiliation.

"Is it the girl from the track?" Phil asked, suddenly interested.

"Okay, fine," Hector said. "It does have to do with Mae."

Phil nodded, then stood up and cracked his knuckles. "Older brother duty applies in this case. I've got you. I'll help."

"Wait, you will?" Hector said.

"Of course," Phil replied. "What are older brothers for?"

"Uh, kicking your butt at the track?" Hector chuckled.

"Well, that too."

"So we gotta get that key from Mom," Hector said. "Any ideas?"

"Oh, that's easy," Phil said. He sifted through his desk drawer, then produced a set of keys. He dangled them in front of Hector, making them clink together.

"No way! You have a copy?" Hector said. His eyes focused on the hefty, golden one.

"Yeah, when I turned sixteen, Mom said I earned my own set of keys for the store," Phil said. "And that one day, I'll inherit the business."

"But why didn't you tell me?" Hector said.

Phil clapped his shoulder and stood up. "I dunno, she made me promise to keep it secret. She didn't want you or Luca or Juan getting jealous or something."

"Figures," Hector said. "What *don't* we fight about?"

Phil snorted. "Yeah, Mom knows us pretty well."

They shared a laugh, as only brothers could.

Hector thought it over. "So you'll help me sneak the Zeus Cup out of the store? What if we get caught and you get in trouble?"

"I can take a hit for the team," Phil said. "Let's roll."

19
CERBERUS

"Let's be quick," Phil said as he unlocked the front door at Hero's and led Hector inside.

"Why quick?" Hector asked, glancing around nervously.

"Mom doesn't usually check on the security cam footage," Phil replied, shutting the door quietly behind them. "But you never know. She and Dad are watching football. She could get bored."

"Too bad that dating show's not on tonight," Hector said, following his brother into the dimly lit store. "The one with the girls fighting over that one guy and the roses."

"That doesn't exactly narrow it down." Phil smirked. "Don't they all have that stuff?"

"Point taken," Hector said, heading for the trophy case.

Hector paused reverently in front of the Zeus Cup, displayed in all its glory. He glanced nervously at the security cams mounted on the walls. They each had red lights lit, indicating the cameras were recording.

Phil slipped the heavy key inside the lock and twisted. *Click.*

The door swung open on smooth hinges. Hector reached inside, his fingers wrapping around the trophy. He felt a surge of energy flow through the Zeus Cup into his fingers.

There was power in the Cup—that much was clear. And it seemed to be getting stronger. Maybe because the Celestial Alignment was coming up.

Hector clutched the trophy as they left the store, and Phil locked the door behind them.

"Need a ride?" Phil asked, cocking his head toward his truck.

"Nah, she's meeting me here," Hector lied. "In the park."

Phil nodded. "Have fun, little bro. Just let's make sure we put the trophy back by the morning."

With that, Phil winked, climbed into his truck, and sped off. Rock music blared out as the truck vanished from view. This had been so much easier than Hector could have imagined.

And now he was all alone.

* * *

Hector headed for the park. His camera bag smacked his leg as he walked. He clutched the Zeus Cup in his hands tighter. His plan had better work—or he'd be out of options. He didn't have much time left.

He glanced at the night sky. The sun had just dipped into the horizon, throwing the little downtown area into darkness. All at once, the streetlights flickered on, casting their halos of light.

The full moon was rising. It peeked over the horizon. Soon the Celestial Alignment would hit its pinnacle—and

Hector would be out of time to save Mae. He felt that familiar wave of self-doubt wash through him, but he pushed it away. He had to be a hero tonight—a *true* hero this time.

I have to save her, he thought. *Even if it's the last thing I do.*

When he got to the Hades statue, he studied it. Hades stared down at him impassively. He needed to find the door to the Underworld. And clearly, the Zeus Cup was the key to opening the door. But where was it? He didn't have a clue, or even know where to start.

He gripped the golden trophy while he inspected the statue. He ran his free hand over the smooth facade, but didn't find any clues that would help. Finally, Hector turned his eyes to the sky. The full moon was steadily rising. He missed Mae. She would know what to do, or at least where to start looking.

"Come on, think," he whispered to himself.

He didn't know where the door was. But who did?

That's when it hit him. He didn't know if it would work, but he had to try.

"I summon Pain and Panic," he said. He felt silly even saying those words.

He waited, but nothing happened.

Hector stared up at the statue in frustration. He tried to think about everything he'd read in the book that Mae took from the library. How did Hades summon them?

"Hey, doesn't your master want the Zeus Cup?" Hector said, spinning around. He held the Cup over his head. "So, where are you little monsters hiding? Get over here!"

At first, nothing happened.

But then he felt a sudden zap—like a surge of electricity—emanate from the Zeus Cup into his hands and his body. He could feel the power of the ancient relic.

Poof.

Suddenly, in a puff of pink smoke, Pain and Panic materialized in front of him.

"Hey, we're demons—not monsters," Pain said, sounding insulted. "Get it right, mister."

"Yeah, don't insult us," Panic added in a chipper voice.

"And ya know, we've got other stuff to do. Kidnapping, maiming, torture, et cetera. The Boss Man isn't very patient."

"Summoning isn't instantaneous," Pain added, rolling his eyes. "There's lag time. Don't you know anything about dark magic? What're they teaching you in school these days?"

They both stared at him expectantly with their yellow eyes.

"So whatcha want, Wonderboy?" Panic asked.

Hector hated that stupid nickname now more than ever.

He held up the Zeus Cup for them to see. It caught the moonlight, glinting with golden light. Pain and Panic jumped up and down in excitement.

"Whoo! Lookie here, Wonderboy brought the Zeus Cup," Pain said.

"Oh, give it to us!" Panic swiped at it, but Hector yanked it back.

"Where's the door to the Underworld?" Hector asked, holding the trophy away from their greedy claws. "I want to give it to Hades in person."

"Uh, we're not supposed to tell you that," Pain said, cringing back in fear. "We're just supposed to retrieve the Cup."

"Yeah, his most lugubriousness wouldn't be happy," Panic added.

"Come on, what can he really do to you?" Hector prodded.

"Maim," Pain said right away.

"Torture," Panic added. "Trust us, you don't want to see him really flame out. It's super gnarly."

They both sounded afraid, glancing up at the Hades statue.

"Yeah, why not just give us the Cup?" Panic went on. "That's the deal."

"Yeah," Pain said. "Then we can use the symbols in the marble and open the . . ." He trailed off.

Panic shoved Pain, and they started squabbling. "You weren't supposed to say that!"

"Uh-oh, he knows," Pain said, shoving Panic back.

They both vanished in a puff of pink smoke.

But they'd let a clue slip, and Hector seized on it.

"Symbols in the marble!" he whispered excitedly to

himself, turning to look at the statue again through narrowed eyes.

But he'd examined the whole thing, hadn't he? Of course, he hadn't been sure what to look for. He hadn't seen any symbols, though. Where were they? It was getting darker and darker out and soon he might not be able to find them at all.

He glared up at Hades' face, wishing the god would give him a clue. He remembered how Hades got really angry when he and Mae were snooping around the statue and taking pictures of it.

Maybe he'd gotten upset because the pictures had a clue!

Feeling a rush of adrenaline, Hector pulled out his camera and started flipping through the pictures he'd taken of the Hades statue. He must have captured a clue about the location of the door to the Underworld. That was probably why Hades got so upset and set Hector's camera on fire.

Hector kept swiping until something caught his eye. Could that be it?

His heart thumped faster as he zoomed in on the strange markings on the front of the Hades statue. Some of it looked like Greek writing, but there was something else—etchings that depicted the Celestial Alignment.

He recognized them from the book. He zoomed in closer on the symbols. They led down the front of the statue. He followed them with his eyes, then started back in surprise.

The markings weren't just a clue about where the door was located. At the bottom of the markings, etched into the marble, was the outline of a door.

That's it!

The Hades statue was more than just a normal statue. It actually held the door to the Underworld. That was why Hades could inhabit the marble and bring it to life. The statue was like a gateway to the Underworld, connecting it to this world.

It all made perfect sense.

The Zeus Cup served as the key to open the door for real. That was why Hades wanted it so badly. For now, he was attached to the marble and stuck in Mt. Olympus. But if he could actually open the door . . .

Hector felt a rush of excitement coupled with trepidation, just like before the starting buzzer went off in a big race. He approached the statue with the Zeus Cup.

He hoisted the golden trophy up to the base of the statue, where the strange markings were, and held his breath.

Nothing happened.

"Come on," Hector said, waving the trophy at the doorway. "Open up! I brought the Zeus Cup—I'm the champion and the protector! I won the race and I need to find Hades!"

Still, nothing happened.

Hector's frustration mounted.

"Come on, open up!" he shouted, clutching the Zeus Cup. He dug deeper, searching his heart for why he was doing this. "I'm the champion! And I have to save my friend!"

Everything fell silent, and Hector felt like he'd failed. He turned away in defeat, but that's when it happened—

A bolt of lightning surged out of the Zeus Cup, hitting the statue.

Crack!

A great rumbling erupted, shaking the ground and throwing Hector back. The outline of the door glowed with blue light. Thunder and lightning crackled in the moonlit sky, even though there were no storm clouds in sight.

Hector braced himself, then glanced up at the statue. It rippled with blue bolts of electricity. He felt a great rumbling shake the ground underneath his feet.

Creeaaaakkkkk!

Slowly, almost reluctantly, as if it hadn't opened in a very long time, the front of the statue cracked apart and the door swung open in front of him. It was thick and made of solid marble. Blue light emanated from inside the door, illuminating the steep white marble stairs that led downward as if into a great abyss. Hector couldn't see the bottom.

A horrid stench wafted out from the doorway . . . it smelled of sulfur, like rotten eggs, coupled with the acrid stench of burning.

Ash drifted through the doorway like fallen snow, speckling Hector's hair and dusting the ground. The whole place just felt . . . wrong. Everything in his body made him feel like running away. This was a place of death, literally, and it smelled like it, too.

"No, I can do this," Hector told himself, trying to

steady his nerves. "Even heroes get scared. But they still do what they need to do. That's what makes them *true* heroes."

He had to save Mae. There was no one else who could do it. Besides, it was his fault that Hades had kidnapped her in the first place. He had to help her.

Clutching the Zeus Cup, he stepped through the door and peered down the stairs into the dark abyss below. Suddenly, a three-headed dog lunged at him and gnashed its teeth.

Cerberus.

Hector screamed, dodging out of the way. One head missed him, snapping at his throat, but then a second head lunged for him.

He dodged again, but the third head swung around.

The sharp jaws caught the blue light. The beast howled and snarled, releasing ferocious cries. Hector turned back to flee, but that's when it happened—

The thick door slammed shut with a loud *thud*, sealing him inside the Underworld with the monstrous creature.

He was trapped.

20
THREE HEADS ARE BETTER THAN ONE

With a fierce snarl, Cerberus lunged at Hector again.

Hector dodged the three heads and scrambled up the stairs, using all his superstrength and speed to evade the ferocious, rabid beast.

Hector banged on the door, trying to get it to open back up.

But it wouldn't budge.

It was locked and stayed shut tight. He really was trapped down here. The acrid, sulfurous air choked his lungs. Smoke wafted up the stairs, obscuring the bluish light and making it hard to see anything. He glanced back into the smoke, struggling to see whether the dog was rearing back to make another strike.

The smoke cleared slightly and Hector saw that, sure enough, Cerberus had retracted its heads, preparing to lunge again. Six yellow eyes caught the bluish light while three sets of needle-sharp teeth glinted, ready to devour Hector alive. He wasn't going to get away, but luckily, he'd come prepared.

Hector reached into his camera bag and pulled out a hunk of raw steak. He tossed it at the dog, and the bloody cut of meat hit the stairs, sliding down toward the monster's feet.

"Good boy," Hector urged the three-headed dog. "Dinner's served, go get it!"

With a surprised yelp, Cerberus pivoted and chased after the steak.

The three heads started fighting over it, allowing Hector to slip down the stairs and past the beast into the Underworld—a sprawling underground cavern. Hector took in his surroundings. Warm air wafted up from the cracks in the ground, making him sweat. It smelled like burning and sulfur, too. The light was eerie, otherworldly, and blue-tinged, much like Hades' flaming hair. Rock formations jutted down from the top of the cavern like spikes waiting to impale him.

Hector glanced back at Cerberus, whose heads continued to snap at each other, brawling over the steak. *Just like me and my brothers*, Hector thought, suppressing a grin despite his nerves. He'd stolen the steak from the fridge at home. He just hoped his mother wouldn't be too angry when she discovered that tomorrow's dinner was gone.

Hades was scary, but his mother could be scary, too.

Hector carefully tucked the Zeus Cup into his camera bag, making sure that it was secure. Then he crossed an arched stone bridge over a fire pit, leading him deeper into the Underworld. It smelled like brimstone, sulfur, and smoke. He crinkled his nose in disgust. Everything here felt like it was either on fire or could burst into flames at any moment, just like Hades himself.

Ahead of him flowed the River Styx, winding through the Underworld. He recognized it from the books, too, once again feeling a surge of gratitude for Mae and her idea to research Hades in the library. Books really were like magic. They gave you the power of knowledge, which was the best kind.

Across the river, a giant castle shaped like a skull towered overhead. *That must be where Hades lives*, Hector thought. The castle gave him the creeps. It was lit by blue torches, making the skull look alive with flaming eyes. It was almost as if it was watching him . . . waiting for him.

Hector shuddered, feeling a fresh rush of fear, but he tried to shake it off. He had to save Mae, and he didn't have much time left. The alignment was coming soon.

As he scanned the area for a way across the river, he made the mistake of glancing down into the watery depths, and froze in fear. Ghoulish creatures swirled in the waters, thrashing at him. Their eyes were mournful, and their wailing mouths made them look like they were in a permanent state of torture. They lunged up at him, but the water's surface kept them trapped.

They couldn't get to him.

What are they? Hector wondered, trembling. This place was full of creepy monsters. He needed to hurry. There had to be a way to get to the castle.

THREE HEADS ARE BETTER THAN ONE

Then, in the corner of his vision, something appeared as if from nowhere.

A boat.

It was docked at the edge of the river, piloted by a skeleton waiting to ferry passengers across.

"Yeah, that's *not* creepy," Hector whispered to himself. He started toward the boat, when suddenly, something exploded out of the river and towered over him—

It was Hydra.

Hector had half a second to think before the river serpent lunged. He tucked and rolled away, just missing getting snatched up by the fearsome jaws. If Cerberus was freaky, this monster was way freakier—and had even more heads.

"What's with all the heads?" Hector hissed, recovering quickly. "One isn't enough?"

As if the creature understood his insult, its many heads roared. The creature's breath smelled horrid. Hector cringed back in fear and disgust. "Sorry, your heads are great—"

But clearly the river serpent couldn't take a joke.

It lunged at him again.

"Hey, we can work this out!" Hector tried, somersaulting out of the way just in time. The creature's jaws tore into the ground next to his head, ripping into the rock and cutting into it.

One inch over, and Hector would have been a goner.

He raised his hands. "Look, I just wanna get across the river and talk to your Boss Man," Hector tried, pleading with the creature. "We don't have to fight about it. You can just chill out in your super-nice haunted river and let me go—"

Hydra roared again, cracking open its ferocious jaws.

The creature prepared to lunge at him again.

Hector didn't have a plan this time. But he fell back on a proven strategy, one that kind of summed up his life.

When in doubt—run for it.

Hector sprinted for the boat, using his superspeed. Hydra gave chase, but Hector reached the boat first. The skeleton tilted its head, regarding him with empty eyes.

"Mr. Skeleton, hurry!" Hector said. "Please, take me to Hades!"

"What makes you worthy of passage through the

Underworld?" the skeleton said in a deep, musty voice. Clearly, he wasn't in any rush, either. He sounded bored.

"Uh, worthy?" Hector stammered.

He glanced back over his shoulder. The Hydra reared up behind him, ready to pounce again. The many heads wriggled around. The skeleton leaned on his oar, staring at him impassively through empty eye sockets.

"If you can't prove you're worthy, you must pay the toll," the skeleton continued, unperturbed.

"A toll. What do you mean?" Hector guessed he'd seen a fair number of guests snatched up by the Hydra. It didn't bother him. The Hydra was coming—and it was coming fast.

He had to hurry.

"Uh, I'm the champion—the true hero!" Hector said, fumbling for his camera bag, trying to get it open and reach the trophy. "And I am the protector of the Zeus Cup!"

"Then prove it," the skeleton said blandly.

Hector struggled to get the bag open, then reached inside and gripped the golden handle. His fingers wrapped around it just in time. He held up the trophy. The luminous surface caught the light, throwing off blinding flashes of gold that lit up the cavern.

The Hydra was about to lunge, but instead it reeled back, screeching in pain at the sight of the Zeus Cup. It quickly dove back into the River Styx, swimming deep through the ghoulish souls until it was gone. The water sloshed back into place, rocking the boat.

The skeleton cracked its jaws open and let out a dusty cackle. Or at least Hector thought it was a cackle. He couldn't be sure.

"Well, why didn't you say so in the first place?" the skeleton rasped, using his paddle to turn the boat around. "Hop in, kid."

The skeleton skillfully piloted them down the river toward the stone skeleton castle. Hector couldn't shake the feeling that he was being watched. It gave him the shakes. He peered anxiously into the water. Eerie eyes stared back at him from the depths.

"Wh-what're those?" he asked, pointing at the creatures.

"Mortal souls," the skeleton rasped. "Whose thread of

life has been cut by the Fates. They're imprisoned down here . . . *forever*."

Hector swallowed hard. This was Mae's fate if he didn't save her. Maybe both their fates. Hector dragged his eyes off the souls. He tried to focus on the castle and what awaited him there.

A few minutes later, they pulled up in front of the castle.

"End of the road—or rather, the river." The skeleton chuckled.

"Sense of humor isn't something I expected to find in the Underworld," Hector said, glancing back at the skeleton in appreciation.

"Well, I wasn't always like this," the skeleton said. "I used to be mortal, too. If you're lucky, maybe Hades will let you serve him. Beats being a trapped river soul."

He let out another raspy chuckle, then started back across the river, paddling slowly as the souls drifted around his oar, reaching their ghostly hands out, pleading for help.

But their hands passed through the oar like smoke.

Hector couldn't let that happen to Mae. He turned

away from the river and started up the stairs that snaked into the skull castle. They were smooth, worn down by eons of foot traffic. Blue torches lit the way. The stench of sulfur and smoke grew stronger. The closer he got to the skull's mouth, the hotter it became. Hector started to perspire. The sweat dripped down his face and stung his eyes.

"Haven't they heard of AC in the Underworld?" he muttered to himself.

That was it—he'd officially inherited his dad's corny sense of humor. He knew he should be horrified, but he felt a strange sense of comfort, almost like his family was with him.

He burst into the castle and found Hades sitting in all his godlike glory on his throne hewn out of solid stone. Blue torches glowed on either side of him, matching the blue flames flickering on the top of his head. His yellow eyes fixed on Hector.

"Wonderboy! You made it!" Hades sneered from his perch. "And just in time to save your little friend here."

He gestured to the side of the throne, waving his long fingers. Mae lay there, her hands bound behind her. She struggled against her restraints, trying to get free.

THREE HEADS ARE BETTER THAN ONE

"Hector, you came for me!" she cried.

"How did you find the door to the Underworld?" Hades said, frowning in displeasure. Orange flames licked his forehead as he grew angry.

"Uh, your little minions let a clue slip," Hector said.

"Pain and Panic, get down here!" Hades yelled.

There was a loud commotion, then Pain and Panic tumbled down the stairs and popped back up on their feet.

"Coming, your most lugubriousness!" Pain yelped.

"Pain and Panic, reporting for duty," Panic added with a salute.

Hades snarled at them, flaming even redder. "How'd Wonderboy get in here?" he demanded.

"Uh . . . I dunno," Pain said, glancing at Panic.

"Yeah, no idea how that happened," Panic added. "Zero clue. It's a total mystery—"

"You morons!" Hades said, flaming brighter and hotter.

Pain and Panic morphed into worms. "We are worms." They groveled, writhing around on the ground. "Worthless worms."

"Memo to me," Hades said with a dismissive wave of his hand. "Maim them . . . after I deal with Wonderboy and his little friend here."

Mae shrieked, squirming on the ground and trying to get free. Fear glistened in her wide eyes. She tried to get away from Hades and his flaming head of hair.

"No! Don't hurt her!" Hector said, gripping his camera bag.

Hades stood up, his long black robes blocking Hector's view of Mae. Hector wrapped his hand around his camera bag tighter.

"No matter, give me the Zeus Cup." Hades leered down at him. "And I'll let your little friend go. How does that sound? Plus, I'll forgive you for trying to back out of our deal."

Hector hesitated. He knew that he couldn't trust Hades. He manipulated mortals and was a liar. He'd already proven that. Hector gripped his camera bag tighter, meeting Hades' gaze.

"You want the Zeus Cup?" Hector yelled. "Then catch it!"

With that, he tossed the camera bag at Hades. The bag sailed through the air in a perfect arc.

While Hades lunged for the camera bag, Hector ran to Mae and quickly untied her hands.

"Hurry, we have to run!" he said, dragging her to her feet.

They were both fast as the wind as they sprinted away from the throne room toward the stairs. They flew down the steps, taking them two at a time, and bolted toward the River Styx, but then Mae skidded to a halt. She shot Hector a worried look.

"But the Zeus Cup!" she said, turning back. "We can't leave it behind. You gave it to Hades! Now he'll unleash the Titans and destroy the world. If we don't stop him—"

"Oh, is that so?" Hector said, giving her a sly wink.

"What do you mean?" she said, glancing back. "We have to go back! We can't let him have it."

Hector smirked. Then he showed her the Zeus Cup, tucked under his shirt.

"It's just a little trick I learned from my best friend," he said.

He'd hidden it under his shirt during the boat ride, planning to trick Hades and play dirty to defeat him.

"Wow, you're a true hero," Mae said in amazement. She reached out to touch the outline of the Cup, when suddenly Pain and Panic pounced on Hector, pinning him down.

"Where ya going, Wonderboy?" Pain said.

"Yeah, don't leave the party yet," Panic added with a cackle. "It's just getting started."

They dragged him toward the River Styx, where the ghoulish souls swirled in the dark waters.

"Give us the Zeus Cup!" Panic said, pushing Hector's head toward the murky water, where the souls congregated in anticipation of a new member joining them in eternal purgatory. "Or take a swim in the river!"

Pain reached for the Cup, but Hector struggled, fighting them off.

He got free from the demons for a moment and reached for Mae's hand. She grabbed his hand, holding it tight. "Hurry, let's get out of here!" Hector said, yanking her away.

"Just like it's a race, right?" Mae added with a wink.

THREE HEADS ARE BETTER THAN ONE

They turned to run toward the ferry, when suddenly, a dark shadow stretched over them.

Blue flames erupted into orange, then burned red hot—fiery and angry. Hades was furious. Beyond furious. Livid. Flaming-hot livid. Hades leered over Hector with a creepy, sleazy grin.

His distinctive voice echoed out.

"Looks like Wonderboy's not so wondrous now, is he?"

Seizing on the distraction, Pain and Panic pounced on Hector again, pinning him down helplessly. He struggled against them but couldn't get free. The demons were stronger than they looked, and they had sharp claws. Mae tried to knock them off, but Pain pushed her back.

She fell, hitting her head with a *thud*, and went lifeless.

"Mae! No!" Hector screamed in a panic. "No, let me go!"

He tried to break away, to get to Mae, but he was trapped in the demons' iron grip.

While Pain and Panic held Hector down, Hades towered over him, stretching out his long, thin fingers and reaching for the Zeus Cup, to claim it once and for all.

21
YOUR MOST
LUGUBRIOUSNESS

"**N**o, let me go!" Hector cried, the hope slowly seeping out of him. He stared at Mae, willing her to wake up, but she lay lifeless on the ground, unmoving. That was a bad sign—a very, very bad sign.

"The Zeus Cup belongs to me, Wonderboy!" Hades sneered. His fingers had almost reached the Cup, when suddenly another voice echoed out, strong and fierce.

"Get off my friend!" Mae yelled, swinging a blue torch and hitting Hades over the head.

She'd been faking the whole time!

Seizing on the moment, Hector summoned his last bit

of strength and fought off Pain and Panic, knocking the little demons into the River Styx.

They sloshed around helplessly, clearly unable to swim, while the souls swirled around them hungrily, tugging them down into the watery depths.

But Hades couldn't be defeated so easily.

He rose up in his full, flaming glory. His whole body ignited into bright reddish flames. Hector felt them singeing his body. It was like a wall of heat had hit him, making his flesh burn.

But they still had one more chance to defeat the god.

"Here! Take the Cup!" Hector yelled to Mae. "Save yourself and the world! You're fast—you still have a chance to get away!"

"Wait, wh-what do you mean?" Mae stammered, hesitating. "I can't leave you here."

"I can't save the Zeus Cup—but you can!" Hector said. "It will open the door out of here. You're superfast. You can still get away!"

"Are you sure?" Mae said, wiping away tears.

"No choice," Hector said. "It's the only way to save you—and also save the world."

Hades flamed brighter, lunging for Hector. But before Hades could reach him, Hector tossed the Zeus Cup to Mae, relieved that his final act could protect it from Hades.

Only now, at the end—finally—did he understand what it meant to be a *true hero*.

The golden trophy arced through the air.

He watched as Mae leapt into the air and snagged the Zeus Cup, catching it perfectly, just like he knew she would. She landed gracefully in a crouch, whipping her head back.

But instead of running away, Mae stared at Hector with an evil grin.

She grasped the Zeus Cup in her pale hands. He glanced from her to the trophy. Her face, reflected in the golden metal, looked distorted, almost demonic. She made no move to run away. Why wasn't she running away?

Confusion rushed through Hector.

Instead, Mae sauntered back the other way, toward Hades.

"Wh-what are you doing?" Hector gasped in shock.

22
HADES RULES!

"**M**ae, why aren't you running away?" Hector gasped, unable to believe his eyes. "You can still get out—what're you doing?"

Hades' laugh echoed.

"Oh, Wonderboy, you're so predictable!" he said in his sleazy voice. "Your little friend here was working for me the whole time."

His shadowy figure loomed over Hector menacingly. His dark silhouette was framed by the flickering, bluish torches.

"Wh-what do you mean?" Hector choked out. "She's my best friend. She'd never betray me."

"Oh, you so sure about that?" Hades sneered down at

him. His eyes flicked over to Mae. "My girl, do we have a deal?"

"No, don't do it!" Hector yelled to Mae. "Don't listen to him—he's a liar. He'll unleash the Titans!"

Mae rolled her eyes at Hector, then sauntered over to Hades and handed him the Zeus Cup. Hades grasped the Cup and wrapped his arm around Mae. They both leered down at Hector.

"You know I play *dirty* to win," Mae said smugly. "Just like you. You'd do the exact same thing in my shoes—"

"No, you're wrong about that," Hector stammered, feeling completely betrayed. His heart felt like it was fracturing into pieces. "I trusted you! I thought you were different!"

"News flash, I'm a winner—at any cost," Mae said with a cocky smirk. "You beat me once by cheating, but now you'll never beat me again. After you won the Spartan Run and kept the Zeus Cup, I got an offer that I couldn't refuse . . . from Hades."

"But, Mae, he's going to destroy the world—" Hector started.

"Just some lame god stuff," Mae said dismissively. "I

don't care about that. After you backed out of your deal with Hades, he came to me and promised to make me a rock star. In exchange for helping him get the Zeus Cup back from you and your greedy family."

"Yeah, it really puts the sympathy for the devil into rock music, doesn't it?" Hades said with a fierce grin, making devil horns with his hands. "Kind of has a nice ring to it."

"Mae, how could you?" Hector pleaded. "We're friends."

"We were always competitors," Mae said with a cruel smile. "And now I won, once and for all—and you lost. How does it feel, Wonderboy?"

Hector could hardly breathe. How could he have been so stupid as to trust this person he barely knew?

Phil was right. She wasn't a real friend. He thought that she'd changed her ways, but he was wrong. She'd been lying to him and working for Hades almost the whole time.

Now she was going to be a rock star. Hades was giving her everything that she ever wanted. And Hector would be trapped in the Underworld. Forever.

Hades offered Mae a potion, which she seized eagerly.

"Thank you, my dear," Hades said with a gracious bow. "You may leave us now. The Fates are on their way to deal with *him*." He flicked his hand demurely toward Hector.

Mae turned to leave with her potion, her part of the deal fulfilled. She gave Hector one last conniving look, then turned away and sauntered from the castle, leaving him alone to his fate. Hades loomed over him with a cruel smile. His hair flamed bright orange with red tips.

"Not so strong now, are you, Wonderboy?" Hades said, clutching the Zeus Cup.

He snapped his fingers. Without the Zeus Cup protecting him, Hector's strength started to drain away. He felt his body weakening to how it was before he made the deal with Hades.

But it didn't stop there.

He kept growing weaker and weaker. His strong body shriveled up before his eyes. Out of the corner of his eye, he saw Mae boarding the boat, leaving the Underworld for good.

With another snap of his flaming fingers, Hades

summoned the Fates. They looked like three witches—monstrous, twisted, hunched bodies with beaked noses and roving eyeballs. They cackled horribly, leering at Hector, who lay there weak and helpless with all his power drained.

"Oh, what do we have here?" the first one said.

"A mere mortal, I see!" the second said.

"Ah, his life force is already draining," said the third.

"Right, right, hurry it up!" Hades said impatiently. "I don't have all day. I have a very important appointment to keep with the Titans, you know."

One of the Fates stretched out a string between her fingers while they all chanted together. "Hold that mortal's thread of life good and tight!"

Then one reached out with a pair of scissors. "Incoming!" the Fates cackled as they severed the thread that was Hector's life.

"Nooooooo—" Hector tried to scream, but only a ghoulish whisper left his lips.

Hector felt his soul leaving his body and being sucked down into the River Styx, joining the other trapped souls in their watery purgatory. He tried to fight it, but he had no strength left. The other lost souls swirled around him hungrily, claiming his soul.

The last thing Hector saw before his soul submerged into the watery depths completely was Hades peering down at him, greedily clutching the Zeus Cup.

"Enjoy your new friends, Wonderboy!" Hades cackled. "I'd love to stay and help you get acquainted, but I've got Titans to see, a brother to punish, and a whole world to destroy."

If Hector could have screamed, he would have, but only a soft gasp escaped from his ghostly lips.

THE END

ACKNOWLEDGMENTS

Wow, five books down! Thank you, Disney and dear readers, for giving me the chance of a lifetime to write these terrifying, amazing, iconic characters. I will forever remember this opportunity. It is one of the highlights of my writing life. It will always be so.

I often get asked, *Who chooses the villain*? The answer is that it's always a collaboration with my team. Sometimes, I suggest the villain for the next book; sometimes my team requests that I write a specific character. The thing is . . . all the Disney villains are amazing and terrifying in their own unique ways. Regardless, everyone wins. Hades was the latter. Disney asked me to write him, but I couldn't have been more thrilled to craft this *chilling* new adventure for one of my favorite Disney villains. I've also always been a huge fan of Greek mythology and legends.

Writing Hades (originally voiced magnificently by James Woods) was a true dream job. I loved capturing his snarky voice, and also his minions, Pain and Panic. My original characters—Hector and Mae—also hold a special place in my heart, as does the fictional town of Mt. Olympus, which I created for this story. By now, you know about the *unhappily-ever-afters*. I teared up writing this ending, so I hope it lived up to expectations and you felt it, too.

Of course, I have to thank my amazing team at Disney Books, including my fabulous editor, Kieran Viola, Cassidy Leyendecker, my design team, and Lyssa Hurvitz and my publicity team for working to get the word out to readers (no easy feat these days). Also, thanks to my book agent, Deborah Schneider at Gelfman-Schneider/ICM, and the rest of my rep team at ICM, Gersh, Archetype, and Curtis Brown. It takes a whole dream team to make the Disney Chills and my other books and writing happen, and I am grateful for your efforts on my behalf.

Here's a little secret if you're still reading. So far, this fifth book has been my very favorite to write. Is that because Hades is such a blast? Or simply because this was the fifth, and therefore, I'm settling into the series and enjoying crafting it more? Regardless of the reason, I hope to write more Disney Chills books in the future. So many wonderful villains still left to bring to life in this new universe, so many stories I still wish to tell. Fingers crossed!

Finally, these books belong to you, my dear, sweet readers. Did I give you terrible nightmares? Did you keep reading anyway? Did you need a nightlight even after you closed the pages? I love hearing from you and reading your responses to the books. Your support for my little spooky series means everything, especially in a year that has posed so many challenges.

Hopefully, we will meet on these pages again soon. But in the meantime, as always . . .

Happy nightmares!

—Jennifer Brody (aka Vera Strange)